SAM CRESCENT

EVERNIGHT PUBLISHING ®

www.evernightpublishing.com

Copyright© 2018

Sam Crescent

Editor: Karyn White

Cover Artist: Sour Cherry Designs

Jacket Design: Jay Aheer

ISBN: 978-1-77339-560-9

SAM CRESCENT

DEDICATION

I want to say a big thank you to all The Skulls fans out there. Writing this series has been amazing and I know there are many more books to come. I feel the men impatiently waiting their turn.

To Karyn White for her constant patience with this series and to Evernight for giving it a home. I'm truly grateful to everyone.

SAM CRESCENT

KILLER

The Skulls, 5

Sam Crescent

Copyright © 2014

Chapter One

Kelsey had fucking lied to him. What the fuck was he supposed to think? A husband? Were a bunch a kids about to jump out at him as well? Slamming back another shot of whiskey, Killer relished the burn as the hot liquid slid down his throat. He couldn't deal with what had just happened. Gripping the edge of the bar he pointed to the latest prospect to give him another shot. All he wanted was alcohol to help him deal with the revelation. The sounds of baby cries filled the room. Lash, Nash, Murphy, and fucking Tiny all had their newborn kids around for a fucking barbeque. The new compound was much like the last one only this one had a lot more space. It had been over a year since the attack from The Darkness. Life was back to normal, in his life at least—apart from what he just learned about Kelsey.

"Hey, Giant, how are you doing?" Tate asked, coming to stand beside him. Killer wasn't in the mood for her jokes or even to talk. Out of all of the women, he liked her the least. She was too bossy and didn't deserve Murphy, in his opinion.

"Go away," he said, sipping at another glass of whiskey.

"Ah, what's the matter?"

Gritting his teeth he tried to rid the memory of the jumped up pussy in a suit climbing out of a limo and announcing he was Kelsey's husband. When Killer saw the truth in her eyes, he had gotten on his bike and was out of there. He wasn't sticking around to get muddled up with a married woman.

You love Kelsey. She's not just some married woman.

"Did you and *Kelsey* think it was fucking funny to see me falling for her?" he asked, letting all of his feelings be known as he spoke. The anger refused to go away. All he wanted to do was cause pain and hurt the first person who stepped out of line. For once in his life he'd thought he found the right woman for him. From the moment he'd first set eyes on Kelsey he'd fallen deep. She wasn't like any woman he ever known. Her timid, somewhat shy approach to life humbled him. He loved her curves and her love of cooking.

No, he wasn't a saint. Over the years he'd fucked many women without caring for them at all. Women were a way to get his rocks off, but then he'd met Kelsey, changing all of his thoughts. He tried to be different with her. She was a fucking dental nurse who had gone away to college. With Kelsey, he felt different and wanted to be different for her, to be better. He'd really thought they had a chance. She never made him feel thick or stupid in her presence.

"What the hell are you talking about?"

Several men turned to look at him, shocked. The anger on their faces was evident.

He slammed back the stool, crowding around Tate. She didn't back down once or show any sign of being afraid of him. "Your little fucking friend, were you laughing all this time? How you got Killer to be nothing but a fucking sick puppy dog?"

Tate folded her arms. "Actually, *Killer*, we've got a lot more interesting things to talk about than you."

Grabbing her arms, he hauled her up close. "Then tell me, Tate, why is she fucking married and I'm the last one to know?"

"Get the fuck off my wife," Murphy said, grabbing Killer's arm. He didn't move, only glared at Tate but released her slowly. Turning to Murphy, he saw the rage in the other man's scarred face. No one touched the women, not even in anger, and Killer was crossing the line. Over the last year Murphy had been receiving treatment for the burns he'd gotten from his exploding bike when they were attacked by The Darkness. The scars were a constant reminder of what happened to all of them and the lives lost during that stressful time. Shrugging Murphy off, Killer saw he also held their son in his other arm.

Cursing, he backed away. He wouldn't hurt children, not even when he was angry.

"Have you completely lost your mind? Kelsey is not married. She would have told me, and she doesn't even wear a ring."

"Exactly what I thought, but I just met the man. I don't have a clue who he is. He looks like some kind of businessman." Running fingers through his hair, he turned away not wanting to look at his club. The whole room stared at them. Tiny looked ready to commit murder, but Killer knew that was because of him viciously grabbing his daughter. The club was his family, and they stuck by rules. Lashing out at the women was breaking one of those rules.

"This makes no sense at all," Tate said. "We

know Kelsey. There has to be some kind of mistake. Are you sure you didn't hear wrong? You're not exactly the brightest spark in the box."

"Tate!" Murphy growled at her.

"What? I'm sorry, but it's true. I tell it like I see it, and you've not shown signs of being anything different."

Glaring at the hated woman, Killer folded his arms. "I risked my life protecting yours. You're a real fucking bitch, you know that."

"Old news, buddy."

"Michael Granito, that's his name. I don't know why he's here. I know he's married to Kelsey." Staring around the room, Killer couldn't stomach being in the same room as his friends. He needed to get out before it all threatened to swallow him up.

"I'll talk to her. I'll get it settled, Killer, I promise," Tate said, reaching out to him.

He shrugged her off. "I don't need your fucking help. Fuck this, I'm going out for a ride."

Storming out of the front door Killer walked toward his bike.

"If you think for one minute I'm going to allow you to get on that bike and ride off, you're fucking mistaken," Tiny said.

Killer turned around to see the leader of The Skulls heading toward him. "What's it got to do with you? Stay out of my fucking business."

"You think because I got a couple of kids and I'm married and fucking in love I can't take you? I've been fighting little shits like you all my life."

"You know my name is Killer for a reason, right?" he asked, ready to fight anyone.

"Your name is Theodore, and I can keep using it if you want." Tiny took a step closer, advancing toward him until they stood toe to toe with each other. "You want to try this, then let's do this." Tiny stared into his eyes, waiting.

Killer didn't know if he'd ever be able to beat Tiny. The man had at least fifteen years' experience on him, maybe more.

"I'm not going to fight you," Killer said.

"You a fucking pussy?"

"No, I'm showing my club president respect. My problems have nothing to do with the club. I'm not going to make it start now. You guys are still my family."

Tiny stared at him for several seconds without saying a thing.

"Give me your keys. You can have one of the prospects drive you out of town, but you're not bringing your shit to Fort Wills. You're one of my boys, and I'm not having your death on my conscience. Find a woman, screw her brains out and then leave, and come back here to sort everything out." Tiny always had the final say with the club. This was his way of caring, being the leader they all needed and one of the reasons Killer respected the man.

Killer reluctantly handed over his keys. "I don't want a fucking prospect. They can't handle their own dicks. Send me out Steven. He can think past his own dick."

"You made the right choice," Tiny said.

In one smooth strike, Killer was on his ass. Tiny had landed a punch right to his face.

"Don't ever touch my daughter again like that. You hurt my family and I will end you without a second's thought. You're part of the family, Killer, have been for a few years. The men will wait for your lead in how you want to handle this … marriage. You want to fuck him up, then we're here. We don't attack any of our women, got it?"

Nodding at Tiny, Killer got to his feet waiting for Steven to come on out. He was touched by Tiny's words. In The Lions there was never a sense of family. It was every man for himself. Steven walked out of the clubhouse, swinging the keys between his fingers and whistling. "You prefer my company to a prospect?"

"You got it. If you start ranting at me I'll fucking hurt you."

"Hey, man. I'm a fully-fledged Skull now. I can kick your ass right back if I want to. Tiny's given me permission if you start to piss me off. He thinks it'll be good for you to get your ass handed to you." Steven moved toward the car, laughing.

Out of all the men, Killer liked Steven the best. When the man had gotten shot protecting Angel and Tate, Killer developed a great respect for the man. Blaine was also another man he respected, as he'd been with the two women when they were in danger, taking a bullet as well. Anyone who stood in front of a bullet to protect a woman, no matter who they were, deserved some kind of respect.

Climbing into the car, he pulled the seat back as far as it would go.

"Where we going?" Steven asked.

"A bar with lots of women. Not girls, I want a fucking woman."

Thinking about losing himself inside a woman lost its appeal the further away from Fort Wills he got. The image of Kelsey with her cherry blonde hair and full luscious figure put him off wanting any other woman at all.

The hurt returned thick and fast. Not once did she tell him about her husband hidden away somewhere. The other thing that bugged him was the wealth the man clearly possessed. Was that the draw for Kelsey? She wanted a wealthy man waiting in the wings for when she finally settled down? In all the time they'd been together not once had he gotten that vibe from her. She was always happy with the simple things in life.

Crap. He really couldn't handle thinking about Kelsey in such a way. She'd been the light to everything that darkened his world, and now she was gone.

"If you want to talk about it you can. Kelsey was fucking wrong, man. She should have told you. I won't tell the guys if you cry or snivel around like a little baby," Steven said.

"I've been a biker and a killer for a long time. Don't fucking start with me. Leave her out of tonight."

"I know. I know. I know. You're way older and all that shit. It doesn't mean fuck all to me. We're the same." Steven kept his gaze on the road.

"We're not the same. You don't have a woman waiting for you, and you've not just found out the woman you were wanting belongs to someone else." Killer slammed his fist on the dash in the hope of relieving some of his anger. What the fuck was he supposed to do?

"Hey, don't go taking your anger out on my fucking car. You got an issue with your woman then stop being a fucking pussy," Steven said, yelling. The car came to a sudden stop, and Steven turned to glare at him.

"What the fuck did you call me?" Killer asked.

"A pussy. If another guy has gotten your girl then man up, and then go and claim her. You've got the whole club behind you. They're pissed, royally pissed. You're one of us, and we'll help you. Stop taking your anger out on my car." Steven pulled off again.

Sitting back, Killer thought about what the other man said. Nothing could stop him from going after

Kelsey, but first, he needed to get completely fucking smashed.

****

"Why are you here?" Kelsey asked, storming back into her apartment. She'd tried to catch up with Killer, but he clearly didn't want to talk to her. Running after a bike hadn't been her brightest idea at all. She wasn't into running and was already panting for breath. Michael shouldn't be here at all. He never bothered her. That was their deal.

"I could have the limo chase after him if you wish," Michael said, pointing toward his expensive mode of transportation. She charged past him heading toward her apartment, and now she was waiting for him to answer her question.

Michael closed the door, smoothing down his Italian designed business suit. She imagined everything he wore cost a good fortune. When they first met she'd hated him on sight. Her feelings hadn't changed in the short meetings they had together.

"Why would I need a reason to visit my wife?"

She cringed at the title. They'd been married since she was eighteen and he was twenty-eight. The ten year age gap hadn't bothered her at the time. Nothing had bothered her about Michael. Kelsey hadn't wanted anything from him other than the promise he would leave her alone. All he wanted from her was her name on a marriage certificate. At the time, she couldn't say no as she'd needed what he offered far more than he needed her. Their ceremony had taken place in a small lawyer's office with a priest to bless their wedded life.

"I'm not your wife, Michael. You're not my husband, not really." She walked into her kitchen and put the kettle on. The day at the dentist had been a long one. All of their clients had something to say about The

Skulls, the local ruling biker club. She had done nothing but think about Killer, the one man who got to her in ways no other man ever had.

"A lot of people would say differently. You're given an allowance, Kelsey, so why are you living in squalor?" Michael changed the subject, irritating her.

Closing her eyes she counted to ten. She loved her apartment, and with no intention of being with another man she hadn't thought about finding something bigger. When she'd agreed to marry Michael, he'd paid her a lump sum of money and gave her a monthly allowance. The amount was bigger than anything she ever earned as a dental nurse.

The initial payment she had used to help with her parents' medical bills. She'd not seen her family in a long time, but she knew they were grateful for the money she gave them to leave them living in peace. Kelsey had lied to Tate the first time they met. Her family life had never been perfect at all, far from it.

"I'm not living in squalor." She gritted her teeth as he checked out her books.

"I know you used the money I gave you to pay for your parents' health bills. Since then you've been putting the money back. Why?" He turned toward her, holding one of her cookbooks. Michael had sent it to her when they first got married. She'd refused to go on a honeymoon, and they'd never had sex. In fact, they'd never even kissed either. He'd offered to give her the honeymoon, the wedding package. She didn't want anything from him at all. There was no attraction between them. He didn't need her for sex as he was more than satisfied in that area. That's what he had told her all those years ago.

"I married you because you needed me, and I needed a way out from my parents' debts, Michael. Stop trying to make out we were more than that," she said.

Ten years ago Michael had been about to take her parents' home from them. She recalled begging him, offering to do anything. He refused to listen to her. One week into their packing about to leave, Michael appeared once again, offering her a lifeline she didn't think she'd ever take. If she agreed to be his wife, he'd pay for the house and make sure the deeds were in her parents' names, and he'd also provide her with enough money to give her a brilliant life. At the time she hadn't known Killer at all, and no other man was in the picture. With her weight issues she never intended to settle down with any man. They all wanted slender women whereas she had always been big. She didn't see anything changing in her life. Kelsey had been pretty set in her ways from a young age.

"I was more than willing to make it more. To give you what all girls want." He shrugged, clearly not caring. "You were the one who wanted nothing to do with me." He walked up to her where she stood in the kitchen. "When I found out you were no longer living with your parents I was concerned."

"And it has taken you over five years to come and find out. What do you really want? You made sure I understood you had plenty of women to deal with your *needs.*" She wasn't a fool. Michael was a bastard through and through. Kelsey didn't trust him at all. If it wasn't for him suddenly wanting a wife, he'd have taken her family home away from her. She didn't know why the sudden need had arisen, only that Michael needed her. Kelsey hadn't asked as she was never interested in finding out the truth.

"Why do I have to want something?" he asked.

She felt pushed to her limit. Seeing the hurt on Killer's face would stay with her forever. Kelsey had fucked up bad, and she'd be lucky if he even talked to her again. Pushing hair off her face she glared at him. "Are you seriously asking me that?"

Michael raised a brow, staring at her waiting.

Growing annoyed, she faced him completely, folding her arms under her breasts. "Fine, you want to go all quiet on me then I'll spell it out to you. In the last eight years of our marriage you haven't called on me once. I left my family when I was twenty to live my own life. Not once have you pretended to care. Why now? What the hell is going on?"

He took a step closer until nothing separated them. She felt the heat radiating off his clothing. Her thoughts whirled around wondering what the hell she'd stepped into. Michael reached out, pushing a strand of hair off her face.

Kelsey tensed, pulling away. He caught her, stopping her from moving. There was something dangerous about him.

"I've got business close by. I thought I'd stop by and see you as I've heard a lot of rumors lately. Let's just say I like being married, Kelsey, and I heard news that may not be the case for much longer, your involvement in The Skulls being one of the reasons why."

"What?" She couldn't even think straight. Killer was out there. The one man who made her feel like a sexy woman and she'd hurt him deeply by keeping her married state a secret. There was no way Killer was ever going to forgive her. She tried to pull away from him, but he kept coming back making it hard for her to forget about him. Kelsey loved him. How was she ever going to mend the damage she caused?

"The Skulls are popular, and so is your man, the one lurking about outside. I heard about what was going on down here. For so long you've lived the quiet life of a dental nurse. Your excitement level is nil. Then I heard about Killer and your budding relationship. I hate to be ignored, Kelsey. We've got a deal, and I expect you to live up to it." He cupped her cheek, and she pulled away from him and his touch.

"This is why you've come? To make sure I don't find another man to fall for?" Kelsey left the kitchen trying to put as much space between them as possible.

Michael simply followed her, and she wished she'd bought a bigger house. She didn't know the first clue about the man she married, and she didn't care about him either. Love or any kind of feeling hadn't entered their equation.

"I've kept an eye on you for a long time, Kelsey. Regardless of what you think I do care about you, in my own way, even if you were a means to an end."

Shaking her head, she stared at him as he leaned against the wall. "You mean I let you screw whatever you want without causing problems?"

"You were not in any position to cause problems. This is a matter of business, Kelsey. You'll stay my wife and stick to our contract. I don't give a fuck about the man in your life, but you won't be together," Michael said.

His response angered her.

"What do you know about The Skulls? Why are you here?"

"You're not wearing your ring," he said, pointing at her hand.

"I never wear it." Fisting her palm, she thought about the last time she had worn the wedding band. They'd gotten married and he offered to take her away on a honeymoon, which she declined. When she got home, she stored the ring away in her jewelry box. She'd not taken it out since, not even to sell the damn thing.

Michael lifted his hand up, showing her clearly the gold band she paid for glinting on his finger.

"So, you finally put it on. It doesn't mean anything."

He stepped close once again, removing the band from his finger. "Actually, I wear it all the time."

She saw from the lack of tan along with the ring mark that he indeed wore it all the time.

"You screw everything," she said.

"So, what man wouldn't?"

Michael was not for her. He may wear the wedding band she gave him, but they would never be anything other than on paper. She didn't care about the women he was with and never would.

Heart racing she stared at the band then at him. "I know nothing about you."

"We're married, and I'm not going to let you be taken from me, Kelsey." Again he pushed some hair off her face. Every move he made seemed precise. She didn't trust him one bit. "I know enough about The Skulls and about your man to know I've got a fight. I'm not going to let you leave me, and I've never backed down from a fight."

Before she could stop him, Michael leaned down, claiming her lips. She froze. His lips were hard and unyielding. Her body didn't respond either to his kiss or to his closeness. She'd never liked him. Michael wasn't even trying. She saw through his act.

Killer.

He broke the kiss first. "I see I'm going to have to pick my game up."

"Leave Fort Wills," she said, wanting him gone.

"No, you promised me a lifetime of marriage. You signed the document my lawyers drafted."

Kelsey frowned, watching him walk toward the

front door. "What the fuck are you talking about?" She hated swearing and rarely did, but Michael's words confused her.

"When you signed the pre-nuptial agreement you didn't read it, did you?"

She'd read it, hadn't understood a word and figured there was nothing there to hurt her. At the time she hadn't been able to afford a lawyer to help her.

"No, I didn't read it at all."

Michael chuckled. "Honey, you should have read it. You agreed to be my wife until either you or I die."

"Nothing like that can be written down."

"Really? I got it down, and you agreed with it. You divorce me, Kelsey, and I will make yours and your man's life hard. He's a wanted criminal, you know. Anyway, I've got to go. I'll be at the hotel just outside of town if you want to talk more."

Michael closed the door behind him, leaving the bomb with her.

Chapter Two

The bar was full to bursting with activity. Killer didn't care at all for any of them. Steven parked the car while he ordered beer for the both of them. The whiskey hadn't done anything for him, and during the drive he believed the effects had worn off. Finding a small table off to the corner near the dance floor, Killer took his seat and downed half of his beer before Steven even turned up. He wasn't interested in having a social drink. Killer wanted to drown his sorrows until there was nothing left.

"Parking was a fucking nightmare. You owe me big for this," Steven said, sitting down.

"I'm your passenger. You're the one who brought me here." He looked around seeing the variety of women on offer. Part of him wanted to stop and go to Kelsey while another couldn't deal with what he'd been told.

She betrayed me.

Gritting his teeth, he sipped at the alcohol, knowing the night was going to be a long one.

"You asked for a place to drown your sorrows and forget everything happening in your pathetic life. I did what you asked, and you're repaying me by being a bastard. See what thanks I get." Steven smiled, looking around the room.

"No wonder you got fucking shot. You're too annoying."

Steven tensed, clearly remembering the pain. "I may be annoying, but you love me."

Chuckling, Killer spotted two blondes eyeing up Steven. "You're right about that. Speaking of love it looks like you'll be getting plenty of action by the end of the evening."

"I spotted them when I walked in. They're practically begging to be fucked and fucked well. I'll make them work for it first. I don't want to be too easy."

"You got a problem with fucking women well?" Killer asked.

"Nah, I just bet half the bar's been between those thighs at some point."

"Well, I never thought I'd see the day when you're picky over who you screw." Killer saw the women whispering to each other. Both of them were sweet-butt material. He imagined some of the club men would be all over them like white on rice. None of them held his interest like Kelsey. Fuck, he needed to get her out of his mind.

"I'm not. I'm single and I can screw who I want, but seeing the guys with their women, it makes me wish I got something like that. I mean, I've seen Hardy with Rose, and they're amazing. After everything they've been through they're still in love. Then there's Lash, Murphy, Nash, and just fucking recently Tiny. It makes a man wish for something he can't have," Steven said.

Yeah, Killer knew exactly what the man was fucking talking about, which just hurt even more.

Kelsey, she'd been the one woman he'd thought to settle down with.

Get your head out of your ass. It's not going to happen at all.

Married. He couldn't even for a second believe it to be true, but he knew it was the truth.

Steven grabbed the next round of drinks while Killer sat back watching the women dance on the floor. He wasn't an ugly bastard, and he knew women were attracted to him. A redhead sat at the bar was eyeing him up.

Take her 'round back and bang her. Get all this shit out of your system.

He ignored his thoughts and took the glass from

Steven.

"Do you need me to play nursemaid all night?" Steven asked.

"I don't need you to play it now. Fuck off, have some fun, and leave me in fucking peace."

Several minutes later Steven went and introduced himself to the two blonde women. No one bothered either of them. They both wore their Skull cuts, and their reputations preceded them.

Killer was no longer in the mood to start a fight. All he wanted to do was drown his sorrows and be left alone.

"This place is a little busy for your tastes, isn't it?" Zero asked, taking a seat.

"What the fuck are you doing here?" Killer hadn't invited anyone but Steven along for his pity party.

"You don't own the place, and I can go wherever the hell I chose." Zero glanced around the room, spotting Steven being rubbed up against by two bunnies. "Fuck that guy moves fast. I wonder what we'll call him."

"Can't call him Hardy, but with the way he goes I'm surprised the boy can think."

"He's not that young," Zero said, signaling a waitress.

"Go and get your own beer and stop being a lazy bastard."

"Why? Waitresses are paid for a reason, and I'm going to be a good paying customer." Zero sat back, and even through the crush of people the waitress made her way toward him ignoring the other people in the room who wanted a drink. He slapped her ass when he finished with his order. "God, I love women who are so easy to read."

"What are you doing here?"

"Got sick and tired of the sound of babies crying.

It's so fucking annoying. The club is a place for men and to do what we want. Their old ladies start popping out the brats, and suddenly our club is a fucking crèche." Zero shook his head. "I'm not looking to take care of babies, but I'm looking for a fuck."

"Not even if Sophia asks you?" Killer asked.

The way Zero looked at Sophia showed everyone in the club what the man thought about her. Killer had watched him lusting after the other woman.

"What the fuck you talking about?" Zero grew tense.

"I'm not blind, and everyone knows you've got a thing for Nash's girl." Killer stopped talking as the waitress brought them back more beer.

"If you need anything, honey, call me. I mean *anything,*" the waitress said, walking off.

"I'll be fucking her by the end of the night."

"Are you sure?" Killer asked.

"Look, what I feel for Sophia is no one's business but mine. I'm not going to act on it, and if I want a screw whatever cunt I want, I will. Tiny's already given me the lecture, okay."

"I know. Poaching another brother's girl is going to land you in shit."

Zero glared at him. "Sophia wouldn't give me the time of day. I'm not going to do anything to cause problems. Drop it." His arms were folded, and his defenses were up.

Leaning forward, Killer stared at the other man. "Would you?"

"Would I what?"

"If Sophia responded or gave you any sign that she wanted something from you, would you give in, or would you leave it alone?"

Zero didn't answer for a few minutes. "I'd do

something about it, all right. You want to go running off telling Nash and Tiny how I'd bang his woman at the first opportunity then fucking do it. I'm sick of hiding from this shit." He downed his shot of whiskey then started on his beer.

"What is it about her?" Killer asked.

"What is it about Kelsey? You answer that, and then I'll talk about my woman. Fuck, we were supposed to be getting away from this crap, not talking about it all the time."

Killer stayed silent, staring at the other man.

"See, you talk about your woman, and then I'll talk about mine. Until then, keep your nose out of my fucking business." Zero stared at the dance floor. Steven was gone, and so were the two blonde bunnies.

"What happened to you?" Killer asked, changing the subject.

"What do you mean?"

"When Snitch attacked. Where did you go?"

Over a year ago Snitch and another motorcycle club known as The Darkness had attacked them leaving two of their men dead. One of them was Time, whom Killer had known from his days in The Lions. Killer ended up getting back to Fort Wills where he protected the women who stayed behind the best he could. He knew Tiny had ended up in Vegas and others in hospitals.

"I've got a friend who lives over forty miles out. She put me up and made sure no one knew about my presence." Zero closed down, growing silent. His face shut off all expression. Killer wondered what the hell was going on.

"A woman?"

"Yeah, I'm not some fucking perv, and it's not like that. She's the sister of an old friend." Zero looked out toward the dance floor.

The redhead approached before Killer got another word in.

"Hey, gorgeous, are you planning on asking a lady to dance?" she asked, talking to him.

Killer looked up at her gleaming red hair. She wasn't too young. Her eyes showed too much knowledge for a young woman. Kelsey at the ripe age of twenty-six still showed a great deal of innocence.

Thinking about Kelsey and remembering the smug look on that bastard's face, Killer finished off his beer and grabbed the woman's arm. He didn't lead her out onto the dance floor. Killer took her around the back of the bar.

Behind the bar he saw Steven fucking one blonde against the wall as he fingered the other. Ignoring all feeling inside him, Killer pushed the redhead against the wall.

"Do you want to dance, or do you want to fuck?" he asked. His only interest was in forgetting what Kelsey looked like for a few short minutes. Since he met her, he'd not touched another woman. The thought of being with another woman left him feeling dirty. Remembering the guilt on her face, he no longer cared. She'd betrayed him and was married. There was no way for him to claim the woman he wanted.

"I want to fuck."

Pushing her skirt up her thighs, he felt she wasn't wearing any panties.

"Good." Grabbing the condom from his pocket, he sheathed his cock, found her entrance, and thrust inside.

He'd fuck the memory of Kelsey out of his mind.
****

"You've got a lot of shit to answer for," Tate

said, storming into Kelsey's apartment an hour after had Michael left. Kelsey done nothing but cry since he left. She was trapped in a marriage by a man she didn't even know.

"Have you seen Killer? Have you heard from him?"

"He came to the club after seeing you with your fucking husband. I mean really, Kelsey, why didn't you tell me about him or what the hell was going on in your life?" Tate asked.

"What happened? If he okay? I never meant to hurt him. You have to believe that. I care about him so much." Kelsey stopped herself, feeling the tears well up once more. In all of the years she listened to her mother complain about her weight and her appearance she had never once let a single tear fall. Kelsey knew she wasn't slender or pretty and saw no use in arguing with her mother over the truth. Then Killer, the big giant hulk of a man, finally made her feel some self-worth, and the man she'd married to save her family home arrived. Her life had turned from good to fucking shit in a matter of minutes.

"Really? The club is fucking seething. Killer is one of them, Kels. You've fucked up bad. You look like a fucking whore to them, using one of their own. Murphy didn't want me to come to you, but I know you."

"I swear I didn't mean to lead him on. I know this is all my fault. You have to understand I never expected to meet someone like Killer. Where is he?" Kelsey felt sick to her stomach over what happened. She wished there was some way for her to take back what was happening.

"He's gone to drown his sorrows with Steven. I think Zero followed them as well, but don't worry about them. You've got to tell me about this man you married and didn't tell a fucking soul. What was all that about?" Tate asked. "God, I'm so fucking angry at you."

"You have no right to be angry at me. Killer has a right to be angry, not you," Kelsey said.

"So I mean nothing to you now." Tate glared at her.

Closing her eyes, Kelsey saw Killer's pain once again. "No, you mean something to me. You're my best friend. Killer is the love of my life. I've hurt him, and that was the last thing I want to do. He means so much to me. Why you shouldn't be getting angry is you're my friend, and as my friend you should accept the fact I fuck up. You're a complete bitch at times, but I accept you."

"You think I'm a bitch?" Tate asked.

"You know you are."

"Wow, I can't believe you called me a bitch."

Kelsey stared at Tate for several minutes.

"I'm still mad at you," Tate said.

"I'm sure the whole club is mad at me for what I did to Killer." She hugged her friend, but there was a noticeable difference in their hold.

Licking her lips, she walked into the kitchen, leaving Tate to get comfortable. Tate's anger was more than deserved. She should have said something much sooner. They'd been friends for some time, and she knew Tate spoke her mind about everything.

Making two cups of tea she walked back to find Tate with her feet up on Kelsey's sofa.

"So it's true then about your husband?" Tate asked.

"Yes, it's true."

"You're not wearing a ring. I've never seen you wearing a ring." Tate grabbed Kelsey's left hand, stroking over the naked finger.

"I don't wear a ring. Hold on, I'll grab it for you."

She left the sitting room and went straight for the bedroom. Her jewelry box lay on the vanity table. Opening up the bottom draw she saw the one ring she never wanted to wear. She took it out of the box and carried it back with her. Kelsey placed it in Tate's open palm.

"There," she said, taking a seat beside her.

"Fuck." Tate whistled, looking at the ring. "Your man has got money."

"He's not my man." The only man she ever wanted was long gone now, and it was all her fault for not coming clean about being married. She was a fucking idiot.

"You've got to tell me the story from the beginning and leave nothing out. I'm nosy, and you owe me some kind of explanation about all of this."

Kelsey cuddled a pillow hoping it would protect her against the feelings spiraling inside her. She felt sick to her stomach but knew she had little choice. All of the emotions running through her were her own fault.

"There's nothing romantic in my past."

"I don't care. Look at what happened between Murphy and me. Romance doesn't play into everything. I want to scream and shout at you, but I'm simply going to hold your hand and wait for you to explain." Tate held her hand, offering her some comfort. Kelsey held onto the only friend she had in the world. It was time to finally admit the truth to Tate.

"Over the years my parents had gotten into a lot of debt. I mean a lot. I was so shocked when I heard the amount. I was eighteen and getting ready to apply for college, but we couldn't afford it." She licked her lips recalling the anger she felt when her parents admitted the truth about their ways. Her mother had gambling problems, and when her father found out, he tried to stop it and then became addicted like her mother. Now, they were both able to live without gambling away a single cent, but they had also become ill. She'd not really known her parents at all, and what she did know about them, she didn't like. "I didn't have a clue. They went away when I was seventeen for a week. I didn't think much of it, and it seems they mortgaged the house or something. About a year later, Michael came telling them he wanted payment or we were out." Kelsey laughed. "I didn't have anything to give him, and neither did my parents. They didn't tell me the truth of what was going on. I mean, why should they? I was their only daughter, but it was none of my business."

"I thought your family life was all happy and rosy?"

"I didn't want to burden you with the heavy truth that my family was not all that great. I wasn't raised by bikers, but I wasn't raised by saints either." Kelsey wiped the tears from her eyes. "We couldn't come up with the money, and so he gave us a set time to get out of his home. It was hard, packing everything up and not knowing where you're going to go. I hated every second of it, and I knew I'd make sure it would never happen again. I wouldn't allow myself to be like them."

Tate squeezed her hand.

"Anyway, he came back and said if I married him, signing the prenuptial agreement then he'd give my parents back their house, deal with all of their debts, and then pay me a healthy sum along with a monthly allowance." The tears fell thick and fast. Admitting the truth aloud hurt her deeply. "I sound like a whore." She voiced her own horrid thoughts.

"Did you sleep with him?" Tate asked.

"No, I agreed, and we were married within the month. We didn't kiss or anything. We've not done anything but hold hands. God, I was so stupid. You know there have been days I've not even given him a thought." Kelsey laughed. "He didn't mean anything to me at all. He offered me a lifeline, and like a stupid eighteen year old girl I took it."

"Do you have any idea why he married you?" Tate asked.

"No, I've not got a clue. I'm so stupid. We were not even attracted to each other."

"No, you're not stupid for what you did. You're stupid for not saying anything now. Why didn't you say anything?"

"I don't know. It's too complicated and weird, and I didn't want you to think less of me, and I hated what I'd done and I still do hate what I've done. How can I expect Killer to ever forgive me?" Kelsey asked.

Tate pulled her in close, hugging her tight.

"Do you love your husband?"

"No, I don't even know him. God, what an idiot am I? I don't even know what he does for a living. I know he's wealthy and always pays my allowance. I never spend it, but I've tried to pay back the lump sum I used for college." She laughed. "I could be living like a queen in some deserted island somewhere. Instead, I stay in Fort Wills and risk being shot at."

"I imagine being in a deserted island isn't anything it's cracked up to be like. I bet it's lonely, horrible, and I'll kick your ass if you leave me, Kels. We're BFFs now."

Crying, she hugged her friend close. "You should be hurting me or something."

"No, I'm doing what needs to be done and that's listening to my friend," Tate said. "Besides, I love you, not Killer. I think he's a bit of a moron."

Kelsey cried even though she didn't agree with

Tate's assessment. Killer was a lot of things, but a moron wasn't one of them.

After some time passed and Kelsey made another cup of tea, they sat down together in silence.

"Why don't you divorce him?" Tate asked.

"I would, but he said something I don't like."

"Kels, every woman can get a divorce. It's not the middle ages."

Looking down into her tea, Kelsey wondered what she was going to do. "The prenuptial agreement I signed?" She glanced up to see Tate nod.

"What about it? Rich men and women deal with them all the time."

"Yeah, I know. I, erm, I didn't read mine. I looked it over, was scared, and saw no other choice so I signed it. I didn't even see a future with another man. I didn't consult a lawyer or ask for help, I just signed it. According to him, I signed an agreement to stay married until one of our deaths. I don't even know if that's possible." She wiped a hand down her face trying to clear her thoughts.

"Then employ a lawyer and get him to look through it. I can get Daddy to hire him if you want?"

"Would you do that for me?" Kelsey asked.

"Yes, I would do anything for you. You're my friend."

"He threatened Killer and the club, Tate. I don't know what he knows, but he seems to know a lot."

"Honey, my dad and the club are fine. They'll deal with everything head on. From now on, I don't think you should be keeping secrets like this. This is big news. The club will be pissed, but in time they'll get over it."

Nodding, Kelsey listened to Tate talk about her son and how Murphy's recovery was going. She smiled, laughed, and when night fell she saw her friend out to

Murphy, who was waiting for her.

Closing and locking her apartment door, Kelsey cleaned away the mess from cooking and drinking and took her time in the shower. When she was finished she sat down on her bed thinking over her life since meeting Michael. There was nothing about him in the media to let her know who he actually was. He was a handsome man, and if he was worth a lot of money then surely he would be known for his company and wealth?

She lay down, hoping Michael was lying and he'd leave The Skulls alone. Thinking about Killer brought tears to her eyes. What was she going to do about him? She loved him so much. Covering her face with her hands, she let the tears finally fall. Killer had invaded her apartment and then invaded her heart. She'd done more with him than she ever imagined she'd do in an entire lifetime.

Kelsey really hoped Killer would listen to her when she finally got the chance to explain. She owed him so much.

Chapter Three

Mouth tasting like shit, Killer rolled over feeling the effects of the alcohol he'd consumed the night before. Wiping a hand down his face, he groaned feeling the headache that was sure to kill what the alcohol failed to do.

"Fuck," he muttered, rolling onto his stomach. He was too close to the end of the bed and sank to the floor. No more nights out with Zero and Steven. Those men knew how to party, and toward the end of the night, he'd fucked the redhead multiple times before … shit, he couldn't remember a fucking thing.

When he got back to the club the men had partied with him and partied hard. They had his back, and Killer had felt it for the first time since joining The Skulls. He no longer felt like an outsider looking in.

"There you are. I was wondering when you were going to wake up."

Turning his head he saw the redhead he'd screwed last night entering his room at the clubhouse. He didn't own a place to crash and either stayed at the clubhouse or at Kelsey's. Kelsey, shit, he'd fucked another woman trying to forget about her, and now he felt fucking dirty. Regret filled him as the last night's exploits started to come to him.

"What the fuck are you doing here?" he asked, getting to his feet. The light shining through the window was hurting his fucking eyes.

"You ordered me back."

"I was completely smashed, and you think I wanted you to follow me?" He got to his feet not caring about his nakedness.

"All night you were taking me around back, fucking me or getting me to suck you. You told me I wasn't leaving until you fucked every hole I possessed on a nice warm bed," redhead said.

Scrunching his face up in disgust he looked at her. "And you still followed me back here? Jesus fucking Christ. I need a shower."

He left her alone while he took a red hot shower. Fuck, he'd been with a woman who wasn't Kelsey. Regardless of what happened yesterday he shouldn't have been with another woman. Crap, she was married to another man. What the fuck was he supposed to do? On the one hand he felt guilt, and on the other, he felt justified in finding another woman.

After he scrubbed his body with a hard brush, washed his mouth out and completely rid his body of the night's shame, he climbed out to find Tate standing inside his bedroom with her arms folded.

"What do you want?" he asked.

"Nice shiner you got there."

Touching his face, Killer had forgotten all about the hit Tiny gave him. "Courtesy of your father."

She smirked. "So I've got rid of the two skanks you and Zero brought home. They're on their way, and I think you're a fucking bastard."

"You know what, you can talk shit to your dad and your man, but I don't got to take it. Get the fuck out of my room." He brushed past her not caring that he shoved her a little. Out of all of the women he never liked Tate. She was a first class bitch, but Murphy was in love. Guy was a fucking fool for falling for such a bitch. "You gonna run off to Daddy? Tell him to black the other eye?"

"Is this the real you, Killer? Are you a bastard in real life? Screwing whoever you want and leading women on by bringing them back here? The redhead really thought she was sticking around." Tate followed him in to his bedroom and just kept talking. He wanted her to shut up.

Sitting on his bed, he stared at her wondering what it would take to get her out of his room.

"First, I'm not the one who is married. You shouldn't have gotten rid of my fuck. Now what am I going to do?" he asked, not really in the mood to deal with her.

Tate unfolded her arms, launched a bottle of water at him, which landed on his stomach along with two pills. "Take some painkillers for your head, get dressed, and go talk to Kelsey. You treat her right, or you'll deal with me. She's been a bitch, but she's my friend."

"She's married." He shouted toward her retreating back. Was he the only one who thought the whole married thing was an issue?

"And you've got the whole club supporting you, Killer. They're not rushing to help her out or find out the truth. She's *my* friend. Steven and Zero were there for you last night. When you came back here, living it up, the other men were here for you."

The whole of the club did have his back. They hadn't spoken out against Kelsey as he told them not to bring it up. Steven and Zero had given him a wonderful night. The only problem to him was the woman he brought home. He wished he hadn't.

"Her life is complicated. What happened to her has nothing to do with you or this to make her married. She has a past, and so do you. Okay, her past has leaked into the present, but we'll make it work. She loves you, Killer, not this other guy. Deal with it. I wouldn't bother, but she's in love with you and you're in love with her. Talk to her before you knock up some slut and get saddled with her for the rest of your days." Tate walked out of the room leaving him alone.

He wasn't going to look a gift horse in the mouth. Killer took the two pills and swallowed some water. Shit, he'd have to thank Tate at some point for getting rid of the women. He hated the thought of having to thank Tate. Thinking of what he had done with her sickened him. No, he wasn't going to even try to remember what he did under the influence.

Closing his eyes, Killer wondered if he should just up and leave. The Skulls wasn't his family. They were a club he stuck around with.

Don't think like that.

There was no family for him, but he couldn't stop thinking about Kelsey. The Skulls were his family. They had given him a home and a family even though he'd started out his life in, The Lions. No, he couldn't leave it like it was. He needed to see her, talk to her, get her to explain everything to him.

Getting up, he grabbed a pair of jeans, a white shirt and his leather cut. He ignored the scent of breakfast and Tate's glaring face, heading out toward his bike. On the body of the bike he saw an envelope stuck. Cursing, he stripped it off and opened the letter up. His keys fell out.

Straddling his machine, he turned the ignition over and waited for his beauty to purr to life. Smiling, even with a throbbing headache, he started out of the compound and rode toward Kelsey's apartment.

The wind felt good on his face, and flashes of memory invaded his thoughts. He couldn't think about the other woman. The very thought made him feel sick, exacerbated by all the alcohol he'd consumed.

Parking his bike, he nodded toward a couple of local kids before pressing the button for Kelsey's place.

"Who is it?" she asked. Her voice was so fucking

sweet. His cock thickened at the sound alone. Killer knew he needed to get his act together before he did something stupid. Last night had been a big mistake, one he hoped never to repeat.

"It's me, Kels. Let me in."

The silence between them was deafening. Not long ago she'd have let him up without hesitation.

"Okay," she said, buzzing the door. He walked into the building and went to her place. She lived on the ground floor as she hated heights. Kelsey stood at the door. She wore a large baggy shirt with a pair of string pants. They covered up her curves, and he hated them on sight. Her hair was bound up on her head, the cherry blonde color calling to him to sink his hands in her hair. He noticed her eyes were red and puffy. She blew her nose as he walked toward her.

"Are you sick?" he asked.

"No." She moved out of the way letting him pass. The door closed leaving them alone in her sitting room. He glanced toward the sofa remembering the feel of her in his arms. They'd never gotten further than some heavy petting over clothes. She always refused to get naked in front of him. Killer liked her reserved nature. He had also liked the fact no other man had seen her naked before. Was that all in his head? What man would marry a woman and have nothing to do with her?

He went to the window looking outside wondering what the hell he should say. The last time he'd been here, Snitch had arrived into town and he'd been on guard protecting The Skull women.

"Do you want some coffee?" she asked, catching his attention once again.

"Yeah, I'll have coffee." Removing his jacket he stared at her retreating back. What the fuck should he say? What was the protocol for this?

Dropping the jacket onto the chair, he paced the length of the room. With his bulk it didn't take him long to get tired of pacing. She came back minutes later with two mugs of coffee. He watched her place them each on a coaster on her coffee table. When she was done, she gripped her hands tight together, looking at him. He saw her nerves but didn't have the first clue what to say to her to help.

"How have you been?" she asked.

"You're married?"

She took a deep breath, dropping her gaze. "Yes, I'm married."

Gritting his teeth, he turned his back on her. Fuck, he needed to learn to get his anger under control.

"How long?"

"Since I was eighteen."

Lashing out he sent the display of ornaments and pictures crashing to the floor. He spun toward her. The sound of the shattered glass and porcelain filled the air.

"You've been married nearly eight fucking years, and you didn't tell me you were?" He yelled the words, not caring if he scared her.

Her hands covered her ears.

"It wasn't important," she said, tears falling down her cheeks.

"Not important. You don't think it's important to tell the men you're intending to screw that you're married. What kind of slut are you?"

"I'm not a slut!" She finally shouted back. Her arms slashed the air in front of her. "Don't you dare call me such a thing?"

"I call it the way I see it, babe. You lead men on. You're a fucking cock-tease."

"I'm no such thing." She wiped the tears from her cheeks. "You've got no idea why I married him."

"Then make it clear to me," he said, panting for breath. His anger caught him unawares, and he needed to take time to calm down.

"My family needed the mon—"

"Fucking whore."

He reached down, grabbing the edge of the coffee table and tugged it up. The coffee sloshed out of the cups coating the books, and the wood upended in the opposite direction.

****

Killer trashed her apartment, but she didn't care. The nastiness coming from his lips hurt her far more than any material goods. Unlike her parents, she didn't care about tables or ornaments. He stepped close to her. He was too big for her not to take another step back.

She kept taking a step back until her back was pressed against the nearest wall. Killer's hands went either side of her head. The anger in his eyes startled her. Even with his anger directed at her, she couldn't stop the arousal building inside her. Her pussy pulsed at the closeness of him.

"I'm not a whore," she said, hating the way he saw her.

"You slept with a guy for money. What does that make you?"

"I never said I slept with him. I've never slept with Michael." She cried out as his palms slapped heavily on the wall behind her. He was too strong and could kill her without any effort at all. She knew how he got his name, and he could snap her neck as easily as a twig.

"That his name?"

"Yes, I've never slept with him. I've never slept with any man, Killer. You've got to believe me. I couldn't sleep with *him.*"

He stared into her eyes, and then his gaze dropped down to her lips.

"You've never let a man inside your pussy."

Her cheeks heated. Killer rarely spoke to her so bluntly. *You've hurt him deeply. You deserve this.* "No, I've never been with a man, and I had no intention of ever falling for anyone." She fisted her hands stopping herself from reaching out and touching him.

"Then why did you marry him? We all know marriage leads to something a lot more."

"Not my marriage. He was going to kick my parents out of their home. They'd gone to rehab and stopped gambling, but we had debts. Lots of debts. I can't even begin to tell you how many debts we had. Michael was the one calling them in. He needed a wife and offered to pay everything back providing I became his wife. I didn't think to ask him. I was too busy dealing with the fact I was going to be homeless and so were my parents."

She told him everything going for the finer details rather than the long ones. Kelsey told him the truth about Michael offering her a honeymoon for the sake of it, but she'd turned him down. Neither of them had any real attraction for each other. At first she didn't want to tell him the truth, but he deserved to know exactly what happened in her past with Michael and her marriage.

When she was finished, he stared down at her. The silence between them hurt. They had once been able to talk about anything or at the very least have a silence that felt right rather than stilted.

"Why haven't you divorced him?" he asked.

"I can't. T-Tate is looking into everything for me." She had a feeling it was going to take more than a simple divorce to get rid of Michael.

He leaned down, and suddenly his lips were on

hers. His tongue danced over her lips before sliding inside. She moaned, grabbing onto his shoulders as he suddenly deepened the kiss bruising her lips with his possession.

His hand moved down, grabbing her thigh to draw her leg over his hip. Through his tight jeans she felt the heat of his cock burning through to her core.

This was more than she ever hoped for. Circling his neck, he pulled her up close. She wrapped her legs around his waist, shocked when he held her without making any noise at her weight. He rubbed his cock between her thighs. She felt him get harder as their kiss deepened. Kelsey didn't know if she could sleep with him. Sex was still something she feared. Killer still made her yearn for something more.

Pulling away, she stared down into his eyes.

She opened her mouth ready to speak, but Killer got there first.

"Last night I fucked a woman."

Her heart was torn from her body at his admission. "What?" she asked, unsure if she'd heard him right.

"I went to a bar out of town with Steven and Zero. We had a few drinks, and I fucked a redhead. Tate kicked her out this morning."

Kelsey shouldn't be hurting at the truth he spoke. She was married, but her heart was breaking. He'd been with another woman because of her. *You have no right to be upset.*

"Could you put me down please?" she asked.

He lowered her to her feet. She couldn't look at him. The moment she stared into his eyes, she didn't know what she'd do. Ducking under his arms, she went into her kitchen, grabbing a brush and bucket. She walked toward the mess from her ornament display and some pictures she'd taken of Tate, the baby, and even Killer. Kneeling down, she started to pick up the broken pieces of her life.

He slept with another woman.

Why did she ever think Killer would forgive her? He truly thought she'd been with Michael. There was no way she could be feeling hurt or betrayed. She'd ruined his trust first. Kelsey knew he didn't want to hurt her even though he'd been with another woman. *You should have told him first.* There had been plenty of opportunities for her to tell him the truth. She was the fat girl no one ever wanted to be with. Michael picked her because of the convenience. Killer was dumped with her because of Tate needing protection. She tossed the broken pieces of her life into the bucket, feeling her world breaking with each second that passed. The one thing she did in her life she did it for her parents so they didn't end up on the streets. She had done it for her own peace of mind as well.

Lifting up the display unit she saw all the glass was smashed. There was no way to mend anything. It was all smashed, shattered, and broken, like her.

"I'm sorry. I shouldn't have taken my anger out on your apartment." He made to touch her display unit.

"No, you don't need to do that," she said, holding the unit in place. A piece of glass was sticking out, and she sliced her palm on the sharp piece. Crying out, she pulled her hand away to see her hand was cut open. Cursing, she cupped her palm and walked into the kitchen. There was glass inside the cut. The pain had no effect on her.

"Shit, are you okay?" he asked, coming up behind her.

He touched her back, and she tensed.

"I'm fine. Please, could you leave? I'll clean up

the mess, and I'm really sorry for all the pain I've caused you." What more could she say? Words were a real struggle for her.

"No, you're coming back to the clubhouse with me. Sandy will look after you. Shit, I shouldn't have lost my temper."

"I don't think that's a good idea. Your men probably hate me. I'd rather clean this out myself."

Killer turned her around to face him. "No, you're not going to do this alone." He pulled out a cell phone pressing the device against his ear. "Will you bring a car to Kelsey's apartment? She's hurt herself, and I need Sandy to have a look. Sure."

"They'll be here in a few minutes." He grabbed her hand, going to have a look.

"Will you leave it alone? It's fine. Just a cut."

"I did this." He stared down at her hand.

Pulling away from him, she went back to her work, picking up the debris of her life. "The woman you were with? Is she your old lady now? I don't know what happens. Tate tries to keep club life away from the conversation."

"No, she was just a woman, Kels. She meant nothing to me."

Tears filled her eyes, but for so many years she'd learned to keep the tears at bay. "I rather wish she meant something to you. Your life would be a lot easier without me in it."

"Fuck, don't do this."

She turned to look at him. "I'm not doing anything. I messed up, and you went and found solace in another woman. I'm sorry for hurting you. I hope you believe me. I didn't give my marriage a thought, and hurting you was never my intention. I never thought I'd fall for a man."

He ran his fingers through his hair, looking agitated. "For fuck's sake. You're married, Kels. I saw fucking red when he turned up. You didn't deny it."

"Of course I can't deny it. It's the fucking truth. I married Michael Granito. My family needed the money, and I did what I could to make them happy." She cut off, staring past his shoulder and smiling. The smile didn't reach her eyes.

"What did you want me to do?" he asked, taking a step closer.

Staring at him, Kelsey wondered what she wanted from him. Licking her suddenly dry lips, she turned to stare out of the window. "I didn't want anything from you, Killer. I married when I was eighteen. I never once expected to meet a man who'd want me." She turned back to face him. The tears were thick in her eyes making him blurry. "Don't you get it? I've been a fat woman all my life. I'm fat and ugly. I've been told it enough, and you know what, I believe it. I believe every fucking word I've heard throughout my whole life." The blood from her cut dripped onto her carpet. "Every man and woman I've passed has always found some way of putting me in my place."

"Baby, stop this," he said.

"No, it all makes perfect sense. I mean, why would any man go for me?" She pressed her palm against her chest. The red blood coated the front of her shirt. "I mean, look at me. I'm nothing." Her tears fell down her cheeks, coating her shirt.

Killer walked toward her. She shook him away, but he wouldn't let her go. He tugged her close, and Kelsey saw it useless to fight him. What was the point in fighting him?

I'm nothing.

Her mother's cruel words would stay with her

forever. Over the years she'd been dealt her fair share of hatred. It was time she listened. She may be a married woman, but there was no way she ever intended to be more to Michael than a convenience. Someone knocked on the door, and Killer escorted her out of her apartment.

She felt broken. What was the point of her even living? She had hurt the one man she really loved.

****

Zero stared at Sophia as she handed her daughter to Nash. The woman he'd been with last night had looked nothing like Sophia, and when he woke this morning, he regretted even being with the other woman.

He held a mug of coffee watching her gather up the mess from the party before.

Why couldn't he get her out of his head? He hated Kate, her sister. The other woman had been a whore through and through while Sophia was different. Her curves were sinful, and with his room at the clubhouse being close to theirs, he'd heard her come apart in Nash's arms.

She walked past him, giving him a smile. He sipped his mug as she put the bottles into the trashcan.

"How are you doing today?" she asked, tugging the bag out of the bin.

"I'm good."

"We heard your little party last night. I hope you had fun." Her smile was big and bright as she tugged the bag out of the trash bin.

"It was." He lied so easily.

"I'm going to get rid of this." She nodded to him and then left the bar. Taking his mug of coffee with him, he followed her outside.

Bad move. Turn around and go back.

Still, he followed her outside and watched as she opened the large bin. She was too small to open the bin.

Sipping at his coffee, he opened the lid for her to throw the trash in.

"You're a lifesaver. What would I do without you?" she asked.

"You'd be struggling to put the trash away." He stood close to her, inhaling her sweet scent. Since her pregnancy she'd not lost any of her curves or the sweetness about her. Part of him hated the fact she hadn't changed.

"That's certainly true." She took a step back, tripped over her feet and fell into his arms. Zero caught her to him, brushing his arm across her breasts as he held her. "Great, now add clumsiness to my list of problems and faults." She giggled, standing away from him.

The mere touch of her body against his own made his cock thicken. He wanted a hell of a lot more than a simple touch. Zero wanted to fuck her. Most of his nights were spent imagining what it would feel like to slide his cock inside her sweet, tight pussy, and simply fuck her.

She rested against the wall, tilting her head back to soak up the sun. He stared at her neck, slowly losing his mind. What would she do if he just grabbed her, kissed her and had done with it?

Tiny warned him against poaching other men's women. Sophia didn't belong to him.

"Baby, our angel needs a change. She's, erm, yeah, I'm not changing that," Nash said, coming around the back.

Sophia giggled. "Come on, sweetness."

Zero watched her kiss Nash before smiling at him and then leaving.

"Can't even change a diaper for your woman?" Zero asked.

"You got a smell of that and you'd refuse to as well." Nash leaned against the wall, staring at him. "You still got a torch for my woman."

It wasn't a question, and Zero didn't feel like answering it.

"Everyone sees it, Zero. You're not fooling anyone with the way you look at her."

Turning to face one of his brothers, he stared at Nash waiting.

"Well, come on then. You want to fight me." Zero raised his fists, mocking the action. "I'm sure I can take you."

"I know what you're feeling for Sophia. She has that way about her. When you've been around the club sweet-butts or seen Kate, she's the total opposite." Nash smiled. "She saved me in more ways than she even realizes."

"What are you getting at?" Zero asked.

Nash took a step closer until they were stood toe to toe. "You can look at my woman. You can even speak to her and be in her confidence." Nash didn't blink. The seriousness of what he was talking about didn't leave his face. "But if you ever lay a hand on what's mine, touch her, kiss her, or even so much as tell her what you feel, then I will end you. Sophia is mine. She's my wife, and I will not lose her because you want to fuck her. Am I clear?" Nash asked.

"You're crystal clear."

He watched Nash walk away. When the other man was near the far door, he called out to him. "What will you do if her sweet smiles and talks turn into something more? What happens when Sophia opens her eyes and decides she doesn't love you at all?"

"It'll never happen," Nash said.

Zero was stood outside with his mug of coffee. His drink was cold and unappealing. Cursing, he poured the coffee away and headed back inside. It was time for him to get over wanting a woman he could never have.

Chapter Four

Killer saw Butch wanted to ask so many questions but kept his mouth shut. Kelsey sat in the back of the car nearest the window looking outside. Her hand was cradled against her. The red blood on her shirt stood out contrasting with the white. Tears streaked her cheeks, and the guilt gnawed at him for being the cause. He wasn't stupid. Kelsey's emotions were in fact rather transparent. Killer always knew when he hurt her. The moment he'd told her about the other woman, she looked broken, shattered even.

"How are you doing?" Butch asked.

"I'm fine. You?" Kelsey turned to stare at Butch.

"Good."

The conversation ended. Her face was pale, and he hated it. There was nothing else he could do. The drive to the clubhouse remained silent. Once they parked, Tate walked out with Angel. They clucked around her then helped her inside the clubhouse where Sandy was clearly waiting.

Once alone, he leaned against the car, breathing out a sigh of relief.

"Well, she's a bundle of fun," Butch said, lighting a cigarette.

"I told her about the woman I was with. Fuck, I told her everything, and I lost my temper. She deserves to be quiet." He took the smoke Butch offered, lighting it and breathing in deeply.

"Last I heard you deserved to be angry. Bitch doesn't deserve your apology for treating you the way she did." Butch smiled at the passing sweet-butts. One of them stopped, pressing her body against him. "Go to my room, babe. I'll come and sort your pussy out for you soon."

The sweet-butt walked away shaking her ass.

"I see you're still fucking anything that walks."

"Hey, our men are fast depleting. Someone needs to stay on hand to keep our sweet-butts in line. I've got my pick of the crop. Blaine is always away with Emily and Darcy. I don't even know if that man is part of our club anymore," Butch said.

Blaine had hurt Emily, his woman, deeply, and up until over a year ago he'd not been able to see Darcy, his little girl. Killer knew Blaine would do anything to keep his woman and daughter, even stay out of club business for a while.

"He's part of the club still. He's just got shit to deal with."

"What are you going to do with the married woman?" Butch asked.

"I've not got a clue. I slept with another woman, and I shouldn't have. Fuck, this is not who I am." In fact, Killer felt fucking dirty for being anywhere near the other woman. He couldn't believe he'd let himself screw a woman he didn't even know.

Shaking his head, he finished his cigarette, docking it out.

"Have you met the husband?"

"No, I only saw him in passing. He's not fucking memorable."

Butch laughed. "I knew you'd say that. You shouldn't be feeling guilty. Kelsey is married, and it's not your problem. Oh well, do you want to join me and the sweet-butt? I'm sure she'd be ready for us both."

"Nah, you go on."

He watched Butch leave, heading toward an afternoon of fucking. Entering the club house he saw Hardy and Rose cuddled up together on the far sofa. None of the other women were in sight. Murphy was bouncing his son in a baby chair. The sight of the large man smiling down at the little bundle seemed out of place.

Taking a seat beside him, Murphy nodded his head. "You over your shit yet?"

"I'm getting there."

"I saw your woman. Is she okay?"

"She's not my woman."

Murphy sent him a look. "She's your woman, Killer. I've seen the way Kelsey looks at you. What she did was wrong, but I know you. You can't just give up. Tate's bitching at me. I'll sort her out, but she's all over the place at the moment. She'll see reason soon enough."

"I don't give a fuck about Tate. Kelsey is my concern, and she's married." He sounded out the last word to make Murphy understand.

"I'm not fucking thick, and so what? Tate told me the truth about her marriage. She's not really married in the heart, and the rest can be handled in time. A divorce will work that out. Tate's helping her out. Kelsey doesn't want to stay married to the man."

Murphy's son gurgled, swinging his little fists around.

"Is Tate with her?"

"Yeah, Sandy is bandaging her up now. They're in Tiny's office." Murphy made kissing noises at his boy.

"Where's Tiny?"

"He took Eva and the kids on a trip to Vegas. Alex is sorting out some kind of deal, and they're accompanying him so Eva can see her father." Murphy lifted the cup of coffee to his lips. "Are you here to talk about club business or just to keep yourself from rushing to your woman?"

"It has been a long time since we caught up," Killer said.

"I know. We're a busy lot nowadays."

The scars on Murphy's face reminded Killer of the danger they'd been in a year ago. No one knew how Murphy had gotten out of danger.

"How did you do it?" Killer asked, pointing to his face.

Leaning down, Murphy released his son from the bouncy chair and held him close. "How did I do what?"

"You know what I'm asking."

"How did I escape an exploding bike and get myself to safety?"

Killer nodded.

"I'd already gotten off my bike before it exploded. When it did, I was turned toward it, and the explosion shoved me down to the ground." He stopped to kiss Simon, his son's, cheek. "They were firing bullets on the ground around me. I stayed still, but I think I passed out at some point. The pain was excruciating. I hurt everywhere. You can never tell Tate this. She doesn't know what happened, and she never will."

"Okay, I'm not going to go telling anyone."

"I couldn't move to start off with. The bikes were on the ground, and I couldn't get away. None of them stayed around to see if we were dead. I saw Time and Gunn were dead." Murphy stopped to take a sip of his drink. "Seeing their lifeless bodies will stay with me forever."

Killer couldn't think about Time. The other man, a part of The Lions, had been good through and through. Time's death cut him deeply.

"Someone came down the road. I heard the sound of an approaching car. They stopped, and I was able to raise my hand. The woman helped me out of the debris and into her car. She drove me to the nearest hospital and stayed with me until it was time for me to leave. I couldn't get to a phone. I was passed out. The doctors said I was suffering from shock and what I'd been through."

"Did the woman fall in love with you or something?" Killer asked.

"No, she was a married woman. She just helped me out. Tate comes across as a bitch, and she is a bitch to a lot of people."

Killer smirked. "She's a bitch through and through."

"She's not. I hurt Tate, and she changed. I love her. She's strong, but deep in her heart I see the real her." Murphy smiled, a secretive smile. "When we're alone, I know without a shadow of a doubt how she feels about me. I've got that, Killer. Tate doesn't hold her love back. The scars mean nothing to her." He pointed to the side of his face. "She loves me, and I held her when she cried about what could have happened. I couldn't bear for her to know how close I was to actually dying. If that woman hadn't come down when she did, I'd be dead."

Turning toward Tiny's office, Killer knew part of what Murphy was talking about. If anything happened to his woman, he'd be dead inside. He loved Kelsey, and he fucked up completely. His brothers could say all they wanted about Kelsey being at fault, but it didn't change his own feelings toward what he did. The woman he'd been with meant nothing to him.

Lash walked up, glaring at him. "What the fuck is she doing here?"

"What?" Killer looked around. Angel wasn't in sight.

"Kelsey. I heard what the bitch has done. I don't give a fuck what Angel says, she shouldn't be here." Lash looked ready to commit murder.

"Back the fuck off. She's my woman, Lash. I

mean it, back off." Killer glanced around the clubhouse, and all of his brothers were glaring toward the door where Kelsey was. He'd never seen their anger before. They all had his back. "Why haven't the others said anything?" he asked.

"They're giving you space. They don't like her being here, but you come first, not her." Lash slapped him on the back.

"I appreciate it. Tell them to back off. I love Kelsey, and I will not have anyone say shit to her."

"Will do." Lash moved away going to talk with the others. Killer was shocked by their support but humbled by it.

Turning back to Murphy, he saw the other man was smiling. "What the fuck are you smiling at?"

"You, you look shocked. I told you it was like this, man. We're a family, and she'd hurt you."

"Let it be. This is between Kels and me. I'll sort everything out."

Murphy held his hands up. "I'm on the fence. I love Tate, but I agree with Lash. Bitch should be on her knees begging for you."

Killer shock his head. "It's not going to happen." He didn't like being the topic of their conversation. Quickly changing the subject, he turned the conversation toward Murphy. "You're happier than ever before now," Killer said.

"That I am. Tiny doesn't want to kick my ass for sleeping with his daughter. Here, have a hold of my son." Simon was placed into his arms.

Murphy and Tate's son had the same name as Devil's child. Tate loved the name Simon and had demanded her son be called it, regardless of Devil's son already having the name..

Killer was a large man, and he'd never held a

baby before in his life. "Fuck, Murphy, what do I do?"

"Hold him close. Keep his head secure and smile at him. Don't glare otherwise you'll have him screaming and Tate will kill me. He's got a good set of lungs on him."

Staring down at the sweet innocent face, Killer knew how important it was to have such innocence in his arms. Kelsey held a matured innocence, and he'd squashed on her with his violence and words.

"You'll make it right with Kelsey. Don't feel guilty about what you did. You got it out of your system. Tate is helping you out. She's in talks with the lawyer, and I'm sure they'll be meeting soon enough," Murphy said.

"Thank you."

Murphy burst out laughing. "You look petrified. You're not going to break my boy. He's a big strapping young man."

Killer chuckled. What would Kelsey look swollen with his child? His cock thickened once again. She'd make one amazing mother. Her caring went straight to her core. He'd seen how loving she could be. The lies were another thing. He'd never asked about her being married, and she'd never brought it up. Why the fuck would he bring up her being married? She lived like she was single, and she didn't even own a ring to prove otherwise, at least not that he saw. Shit, he had to get this marriage crap sorted out before he lost his mind. Killer thought about all the sweet things she did that far outweighed the lies. The lies were the biggest problem. She was married. When Tate had been struggling toward the end of her pregnancy, Kelsey made her homemade chocolate ice-cream and waited for her until she finally went into labor.

You ruined everything. You should have stuck

around and heard the truth.

Kelsey was married because of a piece of paper. There was no other reason she and Michael were together. The marriage may be real to the eyes of the law, but it wasn't real between them.

He'd gone and fucked a woman he didn't know without even asking Kelsey about her married state. She never wore a ring, and in all the time they'd known each other, she hadn't talked about Michael once.

How was he ever going to make it up to her?

****

"I'm going to kill that bastard," Tate said, cursing and yelling.

"Will you shut up," Sandy said, glaring at Tate.

"What?"

"I don't give a fuck that you're the fucking princess. Killer has a right to be angry." Sandy glanced at her, and Kelsey felt all the anger directed at her from the doctor. "Killer is part of the club. Your loyalty is with him."

"Fuck him," Tate said.

"No, you don't get to do that. I'm surprised Murphy hasn't told you how it goes. The club comes first, and I'm helping her because I'm a doctor and obligated to. I'm not doing this for any other reason."

Kelsey didn't take offence. She knew she'd fucked up big.

The glares from the other club members had followed her into the room.

Kelsey held her hand up for Sandy to finish cleaning out the glass. "Don't worry about it, Tate. He deserves to be angry. I would be if he was married and been leading me on."

"You've not been leading him on, Kels. For fuck's sake, did he even ask for the truth about why you married him? This Michael person has a lot to answer for." Tate paced her father's office.

"For fuck's sake, Tate. Get it through your thick fucking skull. She has been leading him on. Stop being her friend and see this how it is. Sorry, honey, but it's the fucking truth."

"I know. There's nothing I can say to make up for my actions."

She stared at Sandy. The other woman kept staring at her. Smiling, she tried her hardest to make it reach her eyes.

"Are you okay?" Sandy asked, reluctantly.

"I'm fine."

Inside she was breaking apart and cursing herself. There was so much she should have done. From the first kiss she should have told Killer the truth. She never felt married but on a piece of paper. Michael meant nothing to her nor did the marriage. He wasn't faithful to her. She couldn't stop thinking about all the pain she'd kept at bay over the years. The name calling, the hurtful laughter that filled her thoughts threatened to have her break down in front of these women.

"Do you have any news about the lawyer? I'd really like to talk with him," Kelsey said, changing the discussion.

"He's looking into the prenuptial agreement and also seeing if he can find any news out about Michael without being noticed. Uncle Alex is also seeing what he can find out while he's away in Vegas. We've got this, honey. You'll be divorced in no time and fancy-free."

Kelsey laughed. The noise sounded forced to her. Sandy sat back, looking her in the eye. The other woman still worked at the local hospital but not as much as she used to. Most of her days were spent at the clubhouse or with Stink, another club name.

"I'm worried about you, Kelsey," Sandy said.

"Nothing to be worried about. Killer knocked over my ornament, and I cut myself cleaning up."

"I'm not talking about the cut. You look sad, really sad."

"My husband has come out of the woodwork and is threatening me if I divorce him. I've not got much to be smiling about at the moment."

"You're fat, ugly and useless. Who will want you? You're just a waste of time. Why didn't you die when you were born?"

Words her mother said when she was first down came back to haunt her. When her father was away, her mother took great pride in making her feel less than what she was.

"I don't know if I want you to be alone right now." Sandy pulled the gloves off her hands. "You're going through a lot at the moment."

"I'm fine, Sandy. I've been through a lot worse. I promise you, I'm fine." How many times would she have to say "I'm fine", before people started to believe her?

Sandy kept staring at her. "Okay, I'll leave it for now, but I want you to call me the moment you change your mind and need to talk to someone." The other woman stood, gathered her things and left. Tate stayed in the room. Angel had gone to deal with Lash and their son.

"What's going on, Kels? Sandy doesn't worry for nothing."

Rubbing her temple, Kelsey looked past the woman's shoulder. She wanted some peace and quiet, and at the moment she couldn't get either. Between Tate, Michael, and Killer, she was exhausted.

"I don't know why she's worried. I'm perfectly fine. I'm just tired. It has been a long few days."

"Killer won't hurt you. He's a lot of things, but he's not a dangerous man."

Kelsey smiled. "I know he won't hurt me. He was angry, and he didn't hurt me. This was my own fault. I should have told him the truth and not kept it a secret. Everything that is happening is my own fault. No one is to blame but me. I did this." Standing up, she was ready to leave the clubhouse. "Is it okay if I go?"

"See Simon before you do." Tate offered her a shirt. "Quickly put this on. I love you, but getting your blood over my son is not something I want to remember."

Tugging the stained shirt, Kelsey quickly put the red one Tate offered. The shirt was tight over her fat body. When she got home, she'd take it off and wash it.

They exited the office, and Kelsey followed Tate toward the bar. Killer was holding Simon in his large arms. She stared into his eyes seeing the worry reflected back at her. Dropping her gaze, she waited for Tate to handle the conversation.

"You look adorable, Killer. Terrified but adorable. Come to Mommy." Tate lifted Simon out of Killer's arms. "It's time for you to see Aunty Kelsey. She loves you so much, yes, she does." Tate was talking in a childish voice.

Holding her arms out, Kelsey cradled the little boy to her body.

"You'll never have children. Who in their right mind would bed you? You're useless."

Leaning down, she inhaled Simon's sweet scent hoping her smile stopped everyone from looking too closely at her.

"He's so beautiful," Kelsey said.

"Isn't he just. You'll be having a son of your own, Kelsey." Tate stroked his cheek.

Her words were like a sucker punch to Kelsey's gut. She wasn't going to be having children or anything so enjoyable in life.

"It's time for me to go." She handed the baby back to Tate. "He's perfect." Kelsey looked at Killer. "Will you take me back home?"

"Yeah, I'll take the truck so I can bring my bike back."

Nodding, she waited for him to get up before following him out. She hugged Tate tight to her body.

"Come back soon, honey. You're missed around here."

Kelsey agreed then walked out. Killer was waiting in the truck. She climbed into the passenger side, buckled up her seatbelt and waited.

"I'm really sorry," Killer said.

"You don't need to be sorry about anything. You were right, Killer. I should have told you about Michael a long time ago. This is my mistake, no one else's." Tate may have said the club would miss her, but she'd seen the anger on their faces directed at her. They were all angry at her for her treatment of Killer. He was their brother, and they were only putting up with her because of Killer and Tate. She wasn't an idiot, even though Tate tried to make her feel welcome. Resting her head on her palm, she stayed silent as he drove back through town toward her apartment.

When she saw Michael waiting by her building door, she tensed. Getting out of the truck she waited for Killer to load his bike into the truck. Michael closed the distance, standing beside her. She took a step away, needing some fresh air.

"You gonna piss on her?" Killer asked.

"Do I need to?"

Killer stepped up to Michael.

"Will you two stop it?" she asked, feeling mortified. Both men were incredibly good looking. They were humiliating her in the middle of the street. Anyone who passed them would smirk and point.

"She's not your woman," Killer said, ignoring her.

"No, she's my wife."

"No ring on the finger."

Michael smirked. "There will be. I got here first, Theodore Smith. Back off."

She turned on her heel and left the men to their cock measuring contest. Kelsey wanted a bath and to get out of the tight shirt. Another humiliation to add to everything else she'd been through.

The truck started up, and she felt Michael close behind her. "He's a rather pleasing gentleman," he said.

"Leave Killer out of this. I don't want to know how you know his real name." She walked to her apartment, opening the door and seeing the mess.

"What the fuck happened here?"

"Nothing."

Michael closed the door behind him. She went straight to the shattered pictures and ornament and started cleaning everything away.

"If that bastard hurt you—"

"He didn't hurt me. Why are you still here?" She finished picking up the large pieces and then moved to her coffee table. Michael didn't talk, and she kept working, picking up the mess. She wiped down her shelves from the coffee Killer spilt.

By the time she got her vacuum out, Michael still hadn't said a thing. He picked her unit up and took it out of her apartment. Once she finished cleaning away the little splinters of ornaments left she sat down to look at the pictures. The glass was all gone. What remained were the frames and the pictures. The first one she came to was of Tate. She'd caught the picture at a barbeque in the compound last summer before everything went mental.

Over and over she looked at the pictures.

"How come there are none of you?" Michael asked. He stood behind her looking down.

"I never want my picture taken."

She refused to stand in front of the camera when she clicked away. Who would want her in the picture with them?

Rubbing her eyes, she gathered up the pictures onto the coffee table.

"What do you want?" Kelsey asked.

"I've been informed you're looking for a way out of our marriage. I'm here to tell you to stop looking. You're mine, Kelsey, and you agreed to stay that way. I'm not willing to look for another woman to fill your shoes. I've stayed away, but you're not reneging on our deal."

"You're not telling me you've been faithful all these years," she said, not believing for a second he'd been without sex for eight long years.

"I fuck women when I want, Kels. I will never stop doing what I want. I simply want to keep you as my wife."

Turning in her seat she looked at him. "Why? Why do you want me?"

He frowned. She never argued with him before. This was the first time she'd started asking questions.

Standing up, she faced him, folding her arms underneath her breasts. "You're a wealthy businessman who can have whoever you want. Why are you keeping me around? I'm nothing special. You can have any woman you want. Why do you want me?"

"Because you're mine," he said.

"This is a possession thing. Someone wants me, and now you want me? God, what is with you men? Why can't you just leave me out of all of your crap?"

"You really don't see your value, do you?" His searing gaze made her feel uncomfortable.

"Please leave," she said. She no longer wanted to have this discussion with him. Michael's actions were like a locked vault, and he would only let her see why he wanted her when he was ready.

"Fine, I'll go, but I promise you, Kelsey, this is not over."

She flinched when he slammed the door closed. Her life sucked. Memories of her mother's hard words had been driving her crazy all day. Would she ever get away from what her mother did to her?

Tugging the shirt from her body, she walked into the bathroom needing to wash her body. Her life had gone to shit, and she couldn't handle anything more.

"You're useless, fat, ugly, a waste of space."

Filling the bath with water, she stripped down, staring at her body in the mirror. She was ugly, worthless. No one would ever truly love something so awful. Tears filled her eyes at the remembered pain of her mother's cutting words.

Her mother never lashed out with her hand. The words were the hardest thing to deal with. The first time she met Tate she'd lied about her family. None of them knew the true her.

Tate didn't know what she went through growing up with her mother.

Wiping the tears away, she settled in the bath. The names she'd been called went around and around inside her head.

She couldn't handle it. It wasn't fair at all. Killer deserved someone good, someone who didn't keep secrets. Michael would never tell her the truth. He was a controlling man. Kelsey couldn't handle it anymore.

Climbing out of the bath, she went to her kitchen and grabbed the smallest knife she could find. When she returned to the bath, she remembered all the words spoken to her along with the threat Michael held against her. She tried to find a reason for her to live. What was there for her? Nothing. Killer deserved someone better, someone who wasn't married to a man who refused to let her go. There was one chance for her to leave the world behind. Unbinding her hand, she stared at the cut she had earlier.

The name calling would stop. Everything would stop the moment she took the pain away. Pressing the blade to her skin, she pushed harder.

"You're worthless, ugly, fat."

Sliding the blade down, Kelsey only had one wish, that they scattered her ashes across the ocean.

Chapter Five

Killer nursed his drink back at the clubhouse. The women had left apart from the sweet-butts and Rose. All of the men with children had left as well. Butch had a blonde on his lap, and he was fingering her pussy for all to see. Zero sat beside him, drinking. The other man looked deep in thought. Killer wasn't in the mood for talking and was pleased no one was trying to get him to talk about his feelings and all that shit.

"Kelsey looked really sad today," Hardy said, speaking up. "It's what she deserves leading you on like that."

"Don't, Hardy. I appreciate your concern, but I'm not in the mood. Kelsey, she has her own issues." Killer found himself defending her.

Turning around, he looked at the older man. Rose sat beside her man, sipping from a bottle of water. "She didn't look like herself at all," Rose agreed. "Even though she doesn't deserve any pity."

"Stop it. None of you know the truth about her decision. We had an argument, and I told her about the woman I fucked."

The other men winced. They still wore a frown, and he knew it was directed at Kelsey.

"Come on, guys, she didn't tell him the truth about her married state. He had a right to lose his head for a little while," Butch said, pulling away from the sweet-butt to speak.

"She didn't even tell you the truth?" Rose asked.

"No, she didn't. We've talked a little, but when I first saw Michael I saw the truth in her eyes. I fucked up by screwing with a woman I didn't want. This is between Kelsey and me. I appreciate all of your concern, but please, don't go judging her without knowing everything.

I know I did, and I'll have to live with that mistake for the rest of my life. Everyone has a past. Hers just turned the fuck back up."

"What are you all talking about?" Sandy asked, taking a seat beside Zero. Stink followed behind her signaling for a drink.

"Kelsey. Bitch looked really sad today," Rose said, bringing the other woman up to speed.

"Don't call her a bitch," Killer said.

Sandy nodded. "I've never seen her looking so sad. I know she's fucked Killer up, but I was worried about her, and I didn't want to let her go home. Is Tate with her?"

"No, I dropped her off home. Michael was waiting to have a word with her," Killer said, staring down at his drink. He'd not taken a sip since the drink had been poured.

"She's on her own? I thought someone was going to stay with her."

"What did you see earlier?" Killer asked.

Sandy shrugged. "I'm not a psychiatrist, so I don't know the real signs. She appeared defeated, depressed. If I was at the hospital..." Sandy stopped as she ran a hand down her face.

"If you were in a hospital, what?" Killer tensed as he waited for Sandy to speak. She had all of their attention.

"I'd have her on suicide watch. I don't know why I'm saying that. I know Kelsey. She's a strong woman, besides her issue with lying to everyone. She's got no reason to do that." Sandy wasn't looking at anyone as she frowned.

Killer panicked. Grabbing his phone, he dialed Kelsey's number. The line kept ringing and ringing. "Fuck, no answer." He dialed Tate's number. "Have you spoken to Kelsey this evening?"

"No, I haven't spoken to her since she held Simon. Killer, what the fuck," Tate said.

Disconnecting the line, Killer headed outside.

"Wait, I'm coming with you," Sandy said, running after him.

He heard the commotion in the clubhouse as he left.

"I'm coming with you as well," Stink said, following them all out.

Killer went straight for the truck. He waited long enough for Stink and Sandy to climb inside.

Charging out of the compound, he broke the speed limit trying to get to his woman. Shit, she wouldn't kill herself. Kelsey was not the kind of woman to hide away from everything that was happening. They would get to her apartment to find nothing out of place.

The panic wouldn't stop with his reasoning. He knew something bad had happened. Killer felt it.

"She's going to be fine," Sandy said.

"No, she's not. If you thought she was a fucking suicide risk you should have told me. I'd never have left her." Killer was cursing himself for walking away from her. What kind of bastard was he to just walk away?

Killer parked the truck with the tires squealing. Running to the intercom, he buzzed Kelsey's door. He kept buzzing and buzzing. Nothing happened. There was no response.

"Fuck!" He yelled the word. Using his foot, he started to kick out at the door. He'd pay for the repairs. When the glass wouldn't break, Stink joined him, and together they threw their weight behind smashing the glass.

He unlocked the door and charged toward Kelsey's apartment. His heart was racing, and he'd never been so scared before in his life.

Hearing Stink and Sandy hot on his heels, he pushed all of his weight behind his body and shoved the door open. None of the locks had been put in place, which was not like Kelsey. He told her to always put locks on even in the town of Fort Wills. Why wouldn't Kelsey lock the door?

"Kelsey?" He shouted her name loud enough to be heard throughout the whole apartment. There was no sight of her the moment he walked through the door. Going to her bedroom he saw the bed looked untouched. His stomach was in knots, wondering what he was going to find. The apartment was eerily silent.

Heart in his throat, he entered the bathroom. On the floor was her clothes, and he lifted his gaze up to the bath. The shower curtain was pulled across the bath obscuring his view.

Pulling open the curtain Killer sank to his knees. He pulled Kelsey into his arms. Both of her arms were slit open, the blood leaking out. She was too pale to be normal.

"Kelsey, fuck, what have you done?" He sank his hands into the bath, tugging her close. Reaching for one of the towels he wrapped the cloth around her body.

"Shit, Killer, out of the way," Sandy said, sinking to her knees. "Stink, get on the phone. We need an ambulance immediately."

He watched her press two fingers to her neck. "Her pulse is there, but it's not strong. Fuck, Killer move out of the way."

"Don't fucking tell me to move away." He snarled the words at her. There was no way he'd be leaving his woman again. Fucking shit, she was so pale. There was no way she could survive. The water she'd been in was red.

Baby, what did you do?

Biting his lip, he held onto her, not caring about her naked state even as he tried to cover her with a towel.

"Pull her out of the bath, Killer. I need to stop the bleeding."

"The ambulance is over twenty minutes away," Stink said, cursing.

"She's not going to make it," Sandy said, working. "Grab her a robe. I'm going to bind her arms up. We'll have to take her to the hospital ourselves. We can get there a lot faster without waiting for the ambulance."

Stink hung up the phone and grabbed a robe. Holding her tight in his arms, Killer took the robe from Stink's hands and wrapped it around her as Sandy bound up her arms. His heart was pounding and his head throbbing. Her body was lifeless as he held her.

"Come on, that's going to have to do." Sandy got to her feet, heading out of the apartment.

Lifting her in his arms, he followed them outside. Stink was in the truck firing up the engine. Another car pulled up, and Tate rushed out of the car.

Tears exploded in her eyes. "What the hell is going on? What did she do?" Tate rushed to his side, touching Kelsey.

"Get out of the way, Tate. She needs the hospital, otherwise she's not going to make it." He pushed past her.

"Fine, I'm following. I'm not letting anything happen to my friend." She stormed off to her car. Murphy was driving, and from the look of it, Simon was strapped into the car as well.

Climbing into the truck, Killer cradled her into his arms. Stink took off the moment the door closed.

"She's so fucking stupid," Killer said.

"No, she'd not stupid, Killer. She clearly has a problem. This has nothing to do with her. She's suffering, and we need to be there for her to help."

He ignored Sandy, knowing he would never forgive himself if she died. Kelsey was his world.

They were followed by a cop car. Stink didn't stop.

"When we get to the hospital, you both get out. I'll deal with this fucker," Stink said.

Killer wasn't going to say anything. The only concern was Kelsey.

The tires squealed as Stink brought the truck to a stop right outside of the hospital.

Opening the door, he climbed out, heading inside. He screamed for help.

"Follow me," Sandy said, leading him down a long hallway. Nurses tried to stop him, but Sandy barked orders out. She went into a clear room and grabbed a gown. "Put her down on the bed. I need her file." Sandy started shouting. Placing Kelsey on the bed, he leaned down and kissed her lips.

"You better not leave me, Kels. I fucking love you, and if you die I will never fucking forgive you," he said, breaking apart inside.

"Killer, I need you to get out," Sandy said.

"I'm not leaving her."

"If you don't leave I won't work on her. I need you gone so I can work straight," Sandy said.

"Come on, man, outside," Stink said, appearing in the doorway.

Reluctantly, Killer allowed himself to be led outside of the room. He followed Stink down the long corridor toward the entrance. Tate held Simon cradled to her chest with Murphy stood behind her. Angel was also walking through the entrance with Lash and her son. The

Skulls were turning up to give him the support he needed. They were not here for Kelsey, apart from Tate.

"What the hell happened?" Tate asked. Tears were spilling down her cheeks. Simon wriggled in her arms clearly sensing her distress.

"She slashed her wrists open," he said. Even as he spoke the words, they felt wrong, poisonous even.

"Kelsey wouldn't do something so fucking stupid. She's strong," Tate said, breaking down.

"Baby, give Simon to me. You're upsetting him." Murphy took their son as Tate charged up to him.

"Is this because of you? Did you hurt her? She was fine when she left the clubhouse." She started to land blows to his chest. Killer didn't fight her. Her hits didn't hurt him. He felt torn in two because he hadn't seen a change inside Kelsey.

He was breaking apart inside. The image of Kelsey's pale body surrounded in red tinted water would stay with him forever.

Angel walked forward. Tears were in her eyes. She looked so lost and broken.

"Stop hitting him, Tate. It's not going to help. He's not to blame for this."

Suddenly Tate spun and slapped Angel across the face. Before anyone could stop, Lash caught Tate around the neck, holding on tight.

"Lash, no, don't do it," Angel said, catching the arm that caught Tate. The whole confrontation was going to shit. "Please, everyone is upset. Think about what you're doing." She tried to tug Lash's arm away.

"Step the fuck away from my woman," Murphy said.

The nurses were looking on as if they were some kind of circus act.

"I don't care who you are, Tate. No one touches

my woman, no matter what. You'll fucking apologize for that right now," Lash said.

Tate glared at him, but Killer saw the real tears in her eyes. She turned toward Angel. "I'm so sorry. I didn't mean to hurt you. Please, forgive me. I don't know what the hell I'm doing."

"I know, honey." Angel tugged on Lash's arm. "All's forgiven. Let her go."

Slowly, Lash pulled away. "You forgive too easily," he said. The tension eased slightly.

"I'm sorry, Killer. I have no right to blame you." Tate took a deep breath, closing her eyes. "What the hell happened?" she asked, running fingers through her hair.

"Sandy mentioned some shit about her mood and how she'd want to put Kels under suicide watch. I tried to call her, but she wouldn't answer. She slit her wrists." Killer shook his head recalling the sight of her in red tinted water. He knew he'd never get that image from his mind. Fuck, he needed a drink or something to take his mind of what he just witnessed.

Instead, he walked over to the nurses' station where he needed to fill in the necessary paperwork. Looking down at the list of questions and details, Killer suddenly realized he didn't know a fucking thing about her. He never asked her any real questions about her life, but he hadn't told her anything about himself either.

He took the forms to the waiting room where several people were sitting.

"I can't do this," Tate said. "She's always seemed so strong and calm. I never for one second thought she was capable of killing herself. None of it makes any sense to me. Kelsey is not like this."

Killer couldn't say anything. "We need to get in touch with her husband," he said.

"What?" Tate turned to glare at him. "Why would

you get him involved? Kels wouldn't like it. She hates him."

Pressing the forms against her chest, Killer glared at her.

"Can you answer all these questions?" he asked. "I've not got a clue, and I bet that fucker knows more about her than we do."

Murphy, Angel, and Lash sat opposite them staring. Killer felt stripped to the core at knowing his woman was suffering. Fuck, what if she doesn't make it. He didn't know how he'd live with himself.

"No one knows how to get in touch with him," Tate said.

Someone charged through the front door, and Killer recognized him immediately. "Speak of the fucking devil." Getting to his feet he walked over to Kelsey's husband, who was shouting at the nurses.

"I want to know where my fucking wife is, and I want to know now," Michael said, slamming his palm against the counter. He looked angry and frustrated as he spoke.

"Sir, you're going to have to take a seat."

"No, I fucking won't—"

"Kelsey is in surgery with a damn good doctor," Killer said, speaking up over the commotion going on around them.

"What?" Michael turned to him. "What the fuck are you doing here?"

Tate stormed over. "He's the one who found her."

Michael looked from him to Tate. "Then why don't you tell me what the hell is going on."

"Why are you here?" Killer asked. He needed to stop thinking about Kelsey, pale and lying in the bath surrounded by red tinted water. He'd never stop thinking about her like that. What could have been so horrid to make her kill herself?

"I got a call from one of my men guarding her apartment building. He told me what happened and how you carried her out of there. I left my hotel room to get here as quickly as I could." Michael glared at him.

"She doesn't want you here."

The rest of the hospital fell away as Killer glared at the man opposite him.

"No? Well I'm the one who pays her fees and make sure she's well taken care of." Michael snatched the papers from Killer's hands. "These are all hers I assume?"

Gritting his teeth, Killer nodded, wishing he could wipe the smug smile off the bastard's face. He saw the ring on Michael's finger, taunting him with the prior claim he had over his woman.

Walking away from the man, Killer stood near the secure door wanting to meet Sandy the moment she came out of the room.

Fuck, Kels. You've got to live. I can't live my life without you. I love you. Fucking please, don't die.
****

Zero cleaned away the used bottles and crap from the night before. Most of the men were at the hospital trying to wait for news of Kelsey. He felt sorry for Killer. The man clearly loved her, and now he'd seen her at her most vulnerable.

The door to the clubhouse opened. Zero stopped to watch Sophia walk inside carrying her daughter on her hip. The more he saw her, the more he felt like he'd been hit in the gut by what he couldn't have.

"Let's clean this place up so Aunty Kelsey knows we all love and miss her," Sophia said, talking babyish to her daughter.

He dropped the bottle making her cry out.

"Jesus Christ, Zero, you scared me to death."

"Sorry," he said, holding his hand up.

Her daughter started to fuss, and he watched her place the bag on the floor and rock her.

"I thought everyone was at the hospital or dealing with club business. Nash has gone to help his brother out. Angel won't leave the hospital because of Tate. I heard a lot of stuff went down last night."

Zero nodded, taking in the sight of her beauty.

"Yeah, Kelsey tried to commit suicide. I've not been called for an update, so I'm taking that as good news. Tiny and Eva are on their way back from Vegas." Zero stayed out of the mess. When he got the call from Angel about what was happening, he chose to stay away from the drama. He had far too many problems of his own, including this woman before him.

"I couldn't believe it when Nash told me this morning. Kelsey is so strong. I wonder what set her off," Sophia said, placing her daughter in the crib set up in the corner.

Forcing himself to look away from her, Zero wondered if there would ever be a time when he didn't have feelings for the young woman.

The only real meaning his life had was in trying to avoid this woman. Fuck, he didn't know what he was thinking or feeling anymore. He loved the club, but seeing Sophia everyday was starting to hurt like a son of a bitch. She held such power over him, and from the way she smiled down at her daughter, she didn't even have a clue.

Picking up bottles he started throwing them into the sack he was holding. The bottles smashed with the force with which he threw them inside.

"Hey," she said, touching his arm.

He felt frozen inside from her touch.

Can't have. Can't touch. Can't fucking love.

Pulling away from the feel of her fingers wrapped around his arm he glared at her. "What?"

"What's the matter with you? Did you have feelings for Kelsey?" She frowned, waiting for him to answer.

She really didn't see how she turned him up in knots. He wanted to laugh, shout, scream, and shake her to bloody death. Didn't she have a clue how he felt about her?

"Nothing, I'm fucking fine."

Throwing the bag to the floor he charged toward the door. He needed to get out of here. Being close to her was going to make him do something he regretted.

She belongs to Nash.

"Zero, wait. What's going on?" She ran to the door. The pained look in her eyes struck him deep.

"I need some fresh air. Can't I even have that in fucking peace?"

"I'm so sorry." Sophia dropped her arm giving him the space to disappear.

He walked out of the back to find Steven having a smoke.

"I thought you were at the hospital?" Zero said, grabbing a smoke for himself.

"I was. I came home to give Tiny and Eva the heads-up when they get back."

"Is she dead?" Zero lit his cigarette taking a deep draw from it.

"No. It was touch and go. Sandy said they lost her for a second but brought her back. Killer is beside himself, and her fucking husband is sitting beside him. It's a total fuck up and looks more like a soap opera. No wonder the girl tried to off herself."

Staring at Steven, he shook his head. "You can

fucking talk some, can't you?"

"Fuck off. Besides, it's a good job I'm here so you don't do anything stupid when it comes to Sophia. Bitch isn't worth it, man."

He ignored the advice leaking out of Steven's mouth.

"Fine, ignore me. Shit, I stink. I need to get a bath. Are you sure you can be safe here and not risk fucking your friend's woman?" Steven asked, taunting him on the way back inside the clubhouse.

Zero stared out over the horizon. It was a lovely fresh morning, and the slight breeze ruffled his hair. Fuck, he needed to get his shit together. The Skulls meant everything to him. He didn't want to risk the club for a woman. Sophia was just a woman, and he needed to get it through his thick skull otherwise he'd be out on his ass. There was no way he'd be facing this world alone without his club for support.

Taking out his cell phone, he looked up her number and dialed. She answered on the fifth ring sounding breathless.

"Hello," she said.

"Hey, Prue, it's me."

"Lucas?"

He chuckled. Zero hadn't heard his name in so long. "Yeah, it's me. How are you doing?"

"Me? I should be asking you that. You're the one who came to me a year ago. Are you well? You're not hurt, are you?"

"Nah, I'm good." Her voice was so sweet and he owed her so much, yet he could never repay her for anything. "How are things?"

"Good, it's pretty manic around here at the moment." She went on talking about the fairs, the love she had for picking the fresh fruits and apples. "It's coming up to over ten years, Lucas."

He closed his eyes remembering the pain of the past. "I know, honey. I'll come and see you soon."

"You don't have to come. You didn't last year or the year before that."

"I've got new commitments here. I'll get away from here and try and get up there," he said.

"Lucas, you sound … distracted."

"I've got shit going on down here. In fact I better be going. Take care, Prue. I'll talk to you soon."

Before she said anything else, he hung up the phone. Tears sprang in his eyes at the memory of what Prue created. Fuck, he was turning into an emotional bastard. Talking to Prue wasn't supposed to make him feel like this.

Wiping the tears away from his eyes, he walked back into the clubhouse. Being around Sophia made him forget about his pain and what he'd done.

He stood behind the bar and watched Sophia with her daughter. She was untouchable to him. There was no way for him to get to her, and because of that, they were both safe.

Chapter Six

Kelsey was safe, alive, and fucking breathing. Wiping a
hand down his face, Killer stood up stretching out
his tight muscles. Sandy was talking with
Michael about her care while they were being
kept in the dark. He hated the bastard for what he
was doing. From the look of Sandy's waving
arms she disagreed with him.

She stormed away going straight toward them.

"How is she?" he asked, tensing to hear the bad news.

"She's sleeping at the moment, peacefully I hope."
Sandy ran fingers through her hair. "This is all a
fucking nightmare, Killer. She pulled through, but
I don't think she's stable at the moment."

"Is she awake?"

Sandy shook her head. "No, she's not awake. She's
sleeping. The doctor put her under. She'll be
asleep for a few hours yet."

Michael walked over. "I told you not to say anything."
He folded his arms, glaring at her.

"My loyalty is to The Skulls. You want to get me fired,
go ahead. I never really liked working here
anyway," Sandy said, glaring behind her at
Michael. Killer had a lot of respect for the woman
before him.

"You're not seeing her. I don't care what you meant to
each other. I don't want you near my woman."

Moving Sandy out of the way Killer glared at his
competition. "You really think you can keep me
away?"

"I'm her next of fucking kin. Kelsey is my responsibility.
Not yours."

Taking a step closer, Killer felt all of his rage build up.
He'd love to take a swipe at the man in front of

him. "You want to take this outside, then let's fucking take it." Killer would deal with the bastard like he'd dealt with all of his other enemies in the past.

Michael smirked. "You bikers, you're all the same. You have no respect for the law. I don't see what she does."

"Kelsey never spoke of you," Tate said. "You think you can keep us away you've got another think coming."

For the first time since knowing Tate, Killer was happy to have her at his side. She was a persistent one who eventually got her way.

"Until then none of you are going to see Kelsey. She's not your responsibility. I'll let her know she's loved." Michael turned away about to leave them.

All of his rage coming to the fore, Killer lashed out. He had enough of pompous men telling him what he could and could not have. His love for Kelsey was absolute.

Reaching out, he grabbed Michael's arm landing the first blow to his face. "You want to fuck with me, fine. Don't bring Kelsey into this."

The next blow Michael blocked. The nurses started shouting, and Tate yelled along with them. Before long they were being pulled out of the waiting room and thrown outside. The security guard glared at both of them. "I don't give a fuck what your problems are. This is my hospital, and you'll treat it with respect."

The guard turned away to stop them entering.

"You can't keep me out," Michael said. "My wife is in there."

"Until you settle your problems I'm not letting anyone enter this door. Every part of our hospital is precious. I'm not having you cost us more money."

Wiping the blood from his lip Killer stared at Michael.

"What is your fucking problem?" Killer asked. "I don't know you, and yet you're here pretty much pissing on Kelsey. She just tried to kill herself, and you want to keep me away from her."

"She's my wife. I have a right to care about her and her health."

Killer couldn't argue with him. There was so much he didn't know about Kelsey. Shaking his head, Killer turned away giving the other man his back. He wished he could go back to when Kelsey was in his arms. They'd never gotten naked together, but the heavy petting had been more than enough for him. Her sweetness caught and held him all the time they were together.

She almost died.

The thought of never seeing her again petrified him. A world without Kelsey would be unbearable.

"You throw the fact she's your wife around as if it actually means something," Killer said, turning back to glare at Michael. He wouldn't be pushed aside because of him. Until Kelsey told him she no longer wanted him, Killer wasn't going anywhere. "You've only just come on the scene. Are you telling me you've been faithful to her?"

Michael broke eye contact. "I was prepared to make it more when we first got married. I was more than willing to have her by my side. I never made her any promises I wasn't prepared to keep. She didn't want to have anything to do with me. I left everything alone. All I needed was a wife, and I got it. Kelsey wanted her independence, and who am I to take it the fuck away?"

Spitting blood out onto the pavement he kept his gaze on the other man. "You fucked everything that walked. You can deflect all the fuck you want. You're not in love with Kelsey, and you'll never be faithful to her. Are you a criminal? Kelsey didn't have a clue why you were wealthy."

"She never asked what I did. I own the company her family mortgaged the house with. Also, her family's debts were known to me. I'm a businessman. A legitimate businessman. I own multiple companies, and I invest in small ones that I see turn a profit."

Staring at the other man, Killer could see it. Michael could sure pack a fucking punch. His jaw hurt like hell.

"Why did you marry her?" Killer asked. "If you could have anyone, why her?"

"You really want me to talk about my decision in choosing Kelsey?" Michael laughed.

Killer didn't care. The other man could laugh, mock, or even try to hurt him. He still needed to know the truth. After getting Kelsey's side of the story, he had no choice but to listen to his.

"You're right. I can have any woman I want, and I do, but when I went to see Kelsey about her house she was the first woman who didn't try to use her body to get what she wanted. I was intrigued by her. She doesn't see how pretty she really is, and it makes her sweet, in a humble kind of way." Michael stopped to shake his head. "My father had died years before, leaving me part of our empire. There was a clause that stated I needed to be married by my thirtieth birthday. I could have anyone, but I wanted Kelsey. I've learned through my dealings that a person who owes a lot of money will do anything. She was an easy target, and I was not in the market of trying to woo a woman."

"Kelsey is not like that."

"She was eighteen and desperate. I used her inexperience to my advantage. I know she'd different. The money I've given her over the years hasn't changed her. Her need to protect her parents is what drove her decision. I don't know why. I heard the way they treated her. They were hateful. I thought my father was horrid until I heard them talking to her, treating her like shit." Michael shrugged. "To each their own."

"You're not going to let her go?" Killer asked, keeping him talking.

"No, I'm not going to let her go. Kelsey is my wife and will remain so." Michael buttoned up his jacket. "Now, if you excuse me. I've got to go and make sure *my wife* is in the best possible comfort."

Killer watched him walk away. Every step the other man took made him angrier. He didn't have the kind of money to rival Michael. However, he'd always been able to read people, and there was something in the other man's gaze that struck him when he kept mentioning he was a legitimate businessman.

"What the fuck was that?" Tate asked.

"He's telling me who's boss."

"I hate him. I can't believe Kelsey married him. Not that she had a choice, but still, I fucking hate him. I'm rooting for you, Killer." Tate stamped her foot.

Killer chuckled. "Stamping your foot is not going to achieve anything. We've got to remember she did what she thought was best. She shouldn't have kept it a fucking secret though." After what just happened and almost losing her, Killer couldn't be angry with her. Wiping the blood from his mouth, Killer frowned. "Are you still in talks with your lawyer friend?"

"Yeah, he's trying to find a way out of the prenuptial agreement she signed. So far, no luck." Tate shrugged. "I never knew any of this about her. I hate the fact I don't really know her. I never really tried to know her."

"It can't be helped. We've all got a past, and most of the time we don't want to share them." His past involved killing innocent people for his club's amusement. Killer cut the thought off. Thinking about The Lions would do him no good. Murphy had spoken up for him, and now he was a Skull through and through. "I want you to tell the lawyer to stop."

"What? Why?"

He stared at the door remembering the guarded look in Michael's face. No, he didn't have a degree or a great education, but he knew when people were lying or trying not to lie. "There is something about him I don't like."

"Yeah, he's married to the woman you love."

"It's not just that." He spun around to face Tate. "Tell your lawyer to look at all of Michael's business. Go through the financials and see where the money is coming from."

"You're asking me to break the law."

"Then get Alex to look into it. He'll find what we need."

"What are you thinking, Killer? He's a suave businessman. We can't get him for that."

"I know. Trust me on this, Tate. He's not all he seems. I bet he's got plenty of good businesses that are in fact legitimate, but something is telling me he got

more than he bargained for from dear old daddy."
He started toward the front doors. The guard kept giving
him a warning look.
"Wait, what?" Tate chased after him.
"We're going to beat him at his own game." He pulled
Tate in close knowing she'd tell the others what
he was about to say. "Tell me how a man who is
legitimate would know all about The Skulls and
about me. Michael Granito is not all he makes
out, and I want to know why. It's for the good of
the club."
He walked away, grabbing his leather cut and walking
out of the hospital doors. While Tate was busy
finding out what she could, he was going to do a
little digging of his own.

****

"Your two men are fighting over you. You're a lucky
woman, but I don't like Michael. He's a bastard
through and through. There is something about
him I don't like at all. Killer, on the other hand,
he's got all those muscles, and boy, he looks like
he knows what to do in the sack."
Kelsey heard someone talking, their voices going on and
on about the two men she didn't want to think
about.
One man I don't want to think about.
Her thoughts went to Killer. She was in love with him,
and now she'd never know what it was like to be
with him. Lifting her arm up she stopped as her
arm remained by her side. Frowning, Kelsey
opened her eyes staring up at the white plain
ceiling.
"I'm sorry, honey, the restraints are a precaution." Sandy
came into view.
"Sandy? What is going on?" she asked. Why was she in

the hospital? What the hell was going on?

Even as her thoughts washed over her, the memory of the blade slicing into her wrist caught her unaware.

Fuck, she'd tried to kill herself and failed.

Another failure just like everything else.

Closing her eyes she felt the tears close to the surface. It felt like all she'd done in the last couple of days was cry.

"No, don't cry. I take it you know the truth about why you're here," Sandy said.

"What happened?" Kelsey asked. The moment she'd let the blade slide into both of her wrists, she regretted the action. She'd been too drained and scared to stop what she started.

"You lost too much blood. For a few seconds we completely lost you, Kels. Killer found you with me and Stink. God, I hate that name. He really needs to change his name. Stink is awful, isn't it?" Sandy shook her head.

The sound of a chair being pulled up beside her got Kelsey's attention. Sandy sat down staring at her.

"What time is it?" Kelsey asked.

"It's the following day, and it's late, past eight."

Looking around the room, she frowned once again.

"Why am I here? I thought hospitals have a lot more people." Her thoughts were all over the place. She hated how chaotic her mind was working.

"This is all because of your husband, Michael Granito. No wife of his will get the common hospital treatment," Sandy said, sneering as she spoke. "Can I say he's a fucking bastard?"

"What is he doing here?"

"Kelsey, you almost died. You tried to kill yourself. Killer found you in water tainted with your own

fucking blood. This is a big fucking deal."
Sandy's voice rose.

Wincing, she glanced at the other woman. "Is Killer
okay?"

"My God, what is with you? You can't leave here, Kels.
You've got to be evaluated. Your wrists were
fucking sliced open, and you even did it properly
going up the vein rather than across." Sandy
stood leaning over her.

"I'm sorry." The tears that filled her eyes finally spilled
over. "I don't know what I was thinking."

The lie poured out of her mouth. She was feeling
trapped. Michael turning back up awakened all of
her memories of her parents. Her mother's cruel
words finally got through to her and hurt her
more than ever before.

"Don't cry, Kels. You're loved, and everyone is worried
about you."

"Look at me, Sandy. We barely know each other, and yet
you're the only one here. I'm tied to my bed, and
I'm scared." She couldn't admit to the other
woman that she regretted slitting her wrists the
moment she did it.

"They can't see you. Michael won't let them, and he's
down as your next of kin. He's also paying the
hospital a lot of money to keep them away. Tate,
Killer, and the others are all here, waiting to see
you. Killer left earlier to shower and change. He
had to. He stank and was covered in blood."
Sandy stopped, looking toward the window.

"Michael won't let them in?"

"No, he won't."

"How are you here?" Kelsey asked. Out of all of The
Skulls Sandy was the last person she knew. She
would expect Murphy or Lash to be here before

Sandy.

"I work here, and he can't keep me away. I'm your assigned doctor."

Nodding, Kelsey tried to sit up and failed. Sandy helped her to sit up. "Can the restraints come off?"

"Not yet. We're worried about you."

Gritting her teeth Kelsey turned her head to look toward the window. It was night, and she'd been in hospital an entire day. Kelsey couldn't believe how quickly her life had changed. What would Sandy say if she told her the truth about regretting her decision to end her life?

She felt so fucking stupid, and now she was bound to a bed until someone decided she wouldn't kill herself.

"Once the doctor comes around to do his final assessment of your injuries you'll be moved up to the psych ward where you'll be analyzed. Your treatment will be decided from there."

Kelsey glanced back to see Sandy still stood over her. "I thought you were my doctor."

"I was. Your sweet little husband got me kicked off your case. It doesn't stop me from coming to see you." Sandy gave her a wink. "I imagine he'll be back to see you soon, and I'll be kicked out."

"I don't want you to go." Being forced to deal with Michael while tied down scared the life out of her.

"It's not my decision, honey. I'll talk with some people and make sure you get the best care."

"What the fuck are you doing in here?" Michael's voice boomed through the spacious room.

Closing her eyes, Kelsey tried to cut out the pain of hearing his voice.

"I'm talking with my friend. Back the fuck off. You may

shout and get people to do your bidding, but I'm not most fucking people." Sandy had her hands on her hips facing Michael.

"Don't, please," Kelsey said. She wanted some peace and quiet to deal with what had happened to her.

"She's awake?" Michael asked.

"Yeah, dick-wad, she's a-fucking-wake."

"Please, stop fighting. I can't deal with this." Kelsey would have rubbed her temple if she could lift her hand all the way to her head. Everything was closing in around her.

"Don't stress, Kels. I'll tell Killer you're doing fine." Sandy touched her arm and walked off. Panicking at being left alone with her husband, Kelsey called back to the only woman connected to The Skulls. "What's the matter, honey?"

"Tell him I'm sorry."

"I will. Take care and get well. You've got nothing to worry about. I'll tell him." Sandy left.

Alone with Michael, Kelsey struggled to look at him. After a few minutes passed he walked up beside the bed. She finally looked up at him.

"Hey," he said.

"Why are you keeping my friends away?" she asked, wanting to see Tate but more importantly Killer.

"They're not your friends."

He reached out and stroked her cheek. She jerked her head away, biting down onto her lip to stop herself from crying out.

"I was so worried," he said. His voice was devoid of all emotion. She knew he was lying.

"You're wrong."

"What?"

She stared at the man she called her husband and shook her head. "Tate, Killer, all of The Skulls are my friends. They've been there for me. Last year when this town was invaded by a psychotic murderer, Killer was there taking care of me. Why did you have to come back?"

"We're married, Kels."

"No, I was a convenience. Divorce me, and marry someone suited to you. Stop calling me Kels, and stop treating me like we really know each other. I don't know you." The tears were falling thick and fast. She was scared, panicked, and wanted Killer.

Kelsey wanted Killer's arms wrapped around her, whispering how he felt.

"I didn't call your parents," Michael said.

"Good. Don't." There was no way she'd ever survive her life if her friends met her parents. They were all polar opposites. Her parents didn't care about anyone but themselves whereas The Skulls clearly cared about their own. She'd seen the rough bikers at their worst and at their best. They were hard and partied hard, but they loved their family. No one hurt their family and got away with it. "I want to see my friends." She wanted to see Killer.

"Do you really think I'm going to let that bastard in here to see my wife?"

Growling with frustration, she glared at him wishing she could hurt him with her looks alone.

It was useless. There was no way for her to get through his thick fucking skull.

"I want to see Tate and Killer."

"No."

Staring at the window, Kelsey forced herself to ignore him.

You fucked up, Kelsey. People now think you're insane.

"Are you going to ignore me?" he asked.

She was going to ignore him and anyone who tried to talk to her. Staring at the darkness of night, Kelsey thought about Killer and what it would be like if Michael had never come home. She should have told Killer. Her biggest regret was not telling him the truth. Her life would certainly be easier if Michael never came back.

****

Michael walked out of Kelsey's hospital ward feeling like the worst bastard in the world. From the first moment he saw her, he'd been intrigued by her beauty, but he'd also been pissed by not getting back his money. Kelsey was a pretty girl, innocent in a way he'd never seen before. There was nothing between them, and he didn't want to fuck her either. Her parents took and didn't give him a fucking cent back. She asked for time to pay off her parents' debts, and he respected her for it. Kelsey hadn't been responsible for her parents' debts. The truth was, he had to marry a woman to fit with his father's will. The ultimatum had hit him within days of meeting Kelsey. The way he saw it Kelsey would be easy to manipulate into what he wanted. He liked the freedom of doing what he wanted.

When he first heard about the will his father left, he'd been angry. Then seeing an opportunity to marry a woman who wouldn't make any demands from him had him grasping for Kelsey.

He liked the power of forcing her to do what he wanted.

Also, he liked being a married man. The gold-digging whores stayed well away. People didn't mess with him, and it gave him the edge when no one knew where to look. He made sure no one knew about Kelsey. If they ever found out the true identity of his wife she'd be in danger.

His father had given him an ultimatum, and Kelsey was the only safe woman he could think of to marry. Besides the usual legitimate businesses, Michael had inherited something far worse, and he hoped to never let it touch Kelsey. He'd married her to gain his full inheritance, but he wasn't prepared to have her death on his conscience. Michael hadn't liked everything he inherited, but there was nothing he could do to stop it.

The only reason he was in Fort Wills was because of his *other* business. While he was here he always intended to visit Kelsey and remind her of their bargain. Hearing about her involvement with The Skulls hadn't helped matters. The last thing he needed was the club looking into him.

Glancing at his watch, he saw it was time to leave. If his business associates knew who Kelsey was, she'd be in danger. He was risking fucking everything to keep her hidden, his own life as well.

Leaving the hospital he caught sight of Killer stood outside smoking. Was he the only one of The Skulls left? With them at the hospital Michael always felt on guard. Killer always looked too deeply. He knew everything about the other man and wouldn't put it past Killer not to look into him. Fortunately, he knew his past and associations were long buried.

"You leaving her for the night?" Killer asked.

"She doesn't want me there. When she's finished here I'll take her away from all this. Probably to one of my islands for her to feel better. Fort Wills is not the place for her to get better. This is a fucked up place, and I don't want her part of it anymore." On one of his islands, he wouldn't have to think about her at all. He didn't love her or want anything else from her, but he didn't want her to die because of him. Michael told her what he wanted her to hear. The life he kept hidden was threatening to spill into their world.

Killer threw his cigarette away standing up to his full height.

Michael didn't scare easily.

"You're not taking Kelsey anywhere. She's my woman, and I will have her off you," Killer said.

"I'd like to see you try." Michael never backed down from a challenge.

"Are you used to getting what you want?" Killer asked.

On guard once again, Michael stared back at Killer.

The other man laughed. "I guess I'll see you around."

Leaving Killer behind, Michael made his way toward his driver. Climbing into the back seat he felt Killer's eyes on him the entire time.

"Do you want me to take you to the next shipment, sir?" his driver asked.

Closing his eyes, Michael nodded. Shit, he wished he'd killed his father before all this shit started.

Chapter Seven

Watching Michael leave, Killer knew his suspicions were right on the mark. There was no way that the other man wasn't dirty in some way. He knew dirty men, and Michael was covered in it. Killer had to admit Michael wasn't happy with his position in life. Whatever it was Tate would get to the bottom of it.

He wasn't leaving the hospital until he saw Kelsey. He'd been going out of his mind with worry for her. No one was going to take his woman away, not even her fucking husband.

"You're going to have to hurry," Sandy said. "Any of the nurses or other doctors see you I won't be able to help."

"I'm grateful for what you're doing. I really am."

"Yeah, yeah, I'm awesome. I know." Sandy led him down a long corridor and went past all of the wards with multiple patients. He didn't look either way. "She's in there. Be careful with her."

"I will." He grabbed the door handle, but Sandy's hand on his arm stopped him.

"No, I mean it. I don't think she intended for it to go this far, but she's still in a delicate condition."

Killer nodded. "I promise. I've got to see her."

"I know." She let out a breath. "If the nurse comes in just ignore her and walk out."

"I've dodged people before, honey."

Sandy smiled. "Okay, take care and good luck." She walked away leaving him alone. The curtain on the door was drawn, and he couldn't see Kelsey. Grabbing the door handle, he let out a breath and entered the room.

She was staring at the window across from her. The only light on came from her side lamp.

Entering the room he closed the door behind her.

"Don't you even trust me to go to sleep on my own?" Kelsey asked. The emotion in her voice tore him apart.

"No, baby. I wanted to make sure you were okay. I had to see you."

She turned, gasping. "Killer, you came."

He watched her jerk on the restraints, whimpering when she couldn't move.

"Hey, don't do that. I'm here." Going to her bedside, he cupped her cheek staring down into her beautiful blue eyes. He kissed her head wishing he could take the tears away. "Don't cry."

"I'm so sorry. I didn't mean for it to go that far. I'm so stupid. Please forgive me."

"Shh," he said. Closing his eyes, he pressed his head against hers. "You don't need to say a thing."

"Yes, I do. I'm so sorry." Her tears were coming thick and fast.

He pressed his lips to hers, silencing her. She whimpered, opening up to his searching tongue. His cock hardened even when he tried to put his arousal aside. Kelsey was in no state to deal with a horny man.

Pulling away he smiled down at her. "You gave me a fucking scare there."

"I regretted it the moment I did it."

Killer sat down on the chair beside the bed. He held her hand ignoring the white bandages around her wrists. This was still his woman lying on the bed, and he loved her with all of his heart.

"We'll get everything sorted out, I promise."

"Michael said you wouldn't be allowed to visit me. Did he change his mind?" she asked.

Wiping the tears away from her cheeks Killer shook his head. "He doesn't know I'm here, but it doesn't matter. I'd always find a way to get to you."

"I can't believe you're here. You don't know Michael. He's pretty determined to get what he wants." Kelsey tried to move her arm and growled in frustration. "They think I'm a risk."

He smiled feeling his own tears forcing their way up. Killer felt a lump in his throat at the remembered image of her floating around in her own blood tinting the bath water.

"You're more of a risk than you realize."

"Sandy told me you found me."

"Of course I found you. I'm never going to let anything happen to you. I love you too damn much."

Her tears were falling thick and fast. "You love me?"

"Of course I do, you silly bitch. I've loved you from the first moment we met." Leaning down he kissed her fingers. "I'm a fucking idiot for what I did to you."

"No, you're not." She arched up but couldn't move. "This is awful. How can I hold you after what you've said?"

Getting to his feet once again, he leaned down and embraced her, wrapping one arm around her back while his other kept his body steady while holding her. "I don't need you to say or do anything. I promise. I love you so damn much."

She let out a cry of frustration. "I'm the idiot. I love you, Killer. I should have told you I was married the moment we met. I was so stupid to have not said anything. I know it will never be enough, but I hope with time I can prove to you how sorry I am. I love you, and I don't want anyone else but you. I should have told you the moment I realized how I felt. Instead, I was too scared to tell you the truth about everything. How can you want someone like me?"

He chuckled, loving her words. "Baby, how could

I not want someone like you?"

"I'm fat. I'm useless. You can have anyone you ever wanted."

Fisting his hands Killer forced his anger down.

"Don't ever say anything like that." When he got her alone when she was well and he wasn't terrified he was going to turn her over his knee and spank that fucking ass of hers until it was red raw.

The only hope he held was her admittance she regretted trying to take her own life.

People made mistakes, and he'd make sure he didn't lose Kelsey because of her mistake.

"You're too good for me," she said.

"No, I'm not too good for you, baby. We're perfect for each other. Do you forgive me for what I did?" he asked.

Sleeping with the other woman was something he never wanted to do again. He felt dirty inside and out. Until he made it up to Kelsey he wasn't going to touch her. Killer knew he needed to prove her he'd never be unfaithful.

"Yes, I can't say anything to you. I'm married. How can you even stand to be in the same room as me?"

He wiped more tears from her eyes, cursing as he did. "Don't cry, baby. I love you, and we'll get through this."

"I love you, Killer. He's not going to divorce me or let me get away."

"Baby, I'm a Skull. We always get what we want." He stroked her hair knowing he'd put a smile back on her face.

Sitting with his woman Killer didn't care how much time passed. They didn't need to speak. All he wanted to do was hold her, love her, and take her away from all of this.

"Killer, psst, you've got to leave," Sandy said, calling through the slit in the door. Glancing behind him, he saw her guarding the door.

Standing again, he leaned down kissing her head. "I'll be back before you know it."

"Please, don't let him take over."

"I won't. I promise. The Skulls are behind you, baby." Kissing her head then down to her lips, Killer felt like he was tearing his gut in half at leaving her. "I'll be back."

"Okay, I love you. I'm really sorry, Killer."

"I know, baby. I'll let Tate know you're doing well." By the time he was through with her husband, she'd be seeing Tate herself. No one was keeping Kelsey away from him.

Leaving the room he stood by the door staring at Sandy. "Thank you," he said.

"No problem. You've been with her for over two hours. I distracted the nurses with a case in the Emergency Room. You need to go now for them to do their rounds." Sandy ushered him through the door.

Steven waited outside, smoking a cigarette.

"How is she?"

"Fine. She made a mistake, and now Michael can have her within his clutches. We've got to stop this from happening." Climbing into the passenger side, he waited for Steven to start up the car. "Take me to the clubhouse."

"Tiny and Eva made it back. Angel is looking after all the kids with Tate. Murphy ordered his woman about for a change. You'd have loved to see it."

"There's no way that happened. No one orders Tate around." Killer disagreed. In all the time he'd known Tate, no one got the better of her, not even Murphy.

"It was pretty cool to witness. She was doing the whole ordering about, shouting and shit. Murphy went up to her, grabbed her around the back of the neck, kissed the fucking life out of her and then ordered her out of the clubhouse. Her position is to look after their son, and she was to do it. I've got to give it to him, Murphy has got balls to do that to Tate."

Killer chuckled.

The relationship between Tate and Murphy was something of a mystery to Killer. Still, his friend loved Tate, and because of that, Killer respected it.

"Is Eva there?"

"No, Tiny is. He's sent her home with their kids as well. Alex is back, and they're all waiting for you."

Nodding, Killer sat back. It was late, and he was tired, but until Kelsey was safe in his arms once again he wouldn't rest.

Steven rambled on for the rest of the journey.

Climbing out of the car, Killer headed inside the clubhouse to find all of the men sat nursing a drink. They looked up at him as he entered. Killer walked out of the office looking tired.

"It's about time you turned up," Tiny said. "What have you got to tell us?"

Killer discussed in detail everything from Michael's appearance to Kelsey's suicide along with his suspicions about the Michael's business dealings to the club.

"The lawyer hasn't found anything yet," Murphy said. "To all appearances Michael Granito is a respected member of society. He pays his taxes, and all of his businesses are above board."

"He needs to look a little deeper. I'm telling you that man is hiding something," Killer said, determined to do whatever was necessary to keep his woman protected.

"We need your help in this." He looked toward Alex.

"Me? I'm not some crook-finding service."

"No, you're a Skull through and through," Tiny said. "You've got the men who can make this look more like child's play."

"Fine, I'll do what is needed." Alex walked away grabbing his cell phone and starting a call as he did.

"Right, in the meantime, Sandy is staying in the hospital. Is that okay with you, Stink?" Tiny asked.

"Yeah, she wants to keep an eye on Kelsey. I don't think I could order her away even if I wanted to." Stink spoke up for the first time.

Everyone in the club knew Stink had a thing for the doctor. They all stepped away giving him the time to woo her.

"Good, she's our eyes and ears."

"I'm not leaving the hospital. If he visits her I want to be there to make sure he doesn't try anything funny," Killer said.

"Tate's going as well. She's going to try to see when she can," Murphy said.

Tiny nodded. "I know she's not an old lady, but we're going to treat her as such. I don't agree with what she did to you, Killer. She better make it up to you."

"Thank you, Tiny. I appreciate it, and she will."

"I'm going home to kiss my kids then fuck my woman. Do you think you can keep this place fucking working for the next couple of hours?" Tiny asked.

They all nodded watching their leader leave the clubhouse.

Killer went to his room going straight for the shower. There was no way he would let Michael take Kelsey away from him. He'd kill the bastard with his bare hands if he had to.

****

Kelsey opened her mouth as Michael pressed the spoon to her lips. She was being fed porridge by a man she didn't want. He'd woken her up to a heated call. "Why can't I feed myself?" she asked, hating the humiliation of having him do all the work.

"Doctor wants you to have a psych evaluation before he removes your restraints. Besides, I love feeding you. It's about time I caught up on all my husbandly duties."

She didn't need to use the toilet either. They had a bag for that as well. Kelsey wanted to curse, scream, and rant, but Sandy advised against that. If she came across the wrong way then she'd be restrained to the bed for a lot longer.

Fuck, she really needed to get out. When she got out of the hospital she'd be locking up all of her knives. Would she be able to cut with a blunt knife?

Stupid. Stupid. Stupid.

"Have you seen Killer and Tate?" she asked.

"No." Michael gritted his teeth.

They were out in the waiting room. She bit her lip to stop herself from smiling. Her friends loved her and were not going to be easily forced out of her life.

"What was your phone call about?"

"Business."

Opening her mouth she took the last of the porridge. He placed a straw to her lips, and she sucked the liquid down.

When he leaned down to kiss her lips Kelsey felt guilty the moment his lips touched hers. Her lips, all of her body, belonged to Killer.

"I'm not going to give up, Kels. You're my wife."

"In name only." She turned to look out of the window. What would she give to feel the sunshine on her face?

"We could change that. I've been thinking about our future, and us living apart is no longer ideal. I think we should consider moving in together after all this."

"I'm not leaving Fort Wills."

"Remember the contract you signed. You'll do as you're told."

Fisting her hands, Kelsey felt her temper rising. "I didn't read the blasted contract. Stop throwing it in my face. I've got nothing to come back with. Is that what you like?"

"I warned you to read every word."

"I was eighteen years old. My parents' home was being taken away by you. Debts were mounting. What did you expect me to do?" she asked. Her voice rose along with her temper.

She really hated Michael for the way he held her life over her.

"It doesn't change what's going to happen."

"If the only person I'm allowed to see is you then change the subject. I'm getting tired of listening to a broken record." She stared out of the window hoping he'd take the hint and leave.

Most of her life she'd not been the subject of men's interest. Now, she had two men, both different, and one of them she wanted rid of.

Michael placed a hand beside her head crowding her. "Look at me, Kels."

Reluctantly she forced herself to look at him.

"If you give us a chance we can have so much more," he said.

"I don't want so much more. Why can't you see that?"

"You tried to kill yourself—"

"To get away from you. You hold that bloody

contract over me like a lifeline. I made a mistake in marrying you. Can't you see that?"

He pulled back. She was sure she saw anger reflected in his eyes. Kelsey didn't care. Neither of them was suited to each other.

"Do you want to see your friend?" he asked.

"Yes."

"Then I will go and get her." He stopped at the door, glancing back at her. "Be warned, Kels, I'm not letting you go. There is nothing and no one to stop me taking what's mine, and that's what you'll always be, mine."

He left in the next second. She would never be his.

Tugging on the restraints she let out a frustrated sigh. Getting out of bed would be a welcome escape for the time being. The silence was killing her. She wasn't allowed a television either. The only company she'd been given was Michael.

Sandy snuck in when she could. It sucked. Being in the hospital sucked more than anything else she could think of.

Minutes passed before the door finally opened. Tate stood in front of Michael.

"Honey, Jesus fucking Christ, you scared me, you silly bitch," Tate said, charging toward her.

Kelsey stayed still on the bed as Tate gathered her in close.

"How could you do that?" Tate asked, pulling away.

She was shocked to see the tears pouring down Tate's face. "I'm sorry."

"You should be. I can't believe you did that. What was I supposed to do if you fucking died on me?" Tate glanced behind her. "You can fuck off and leave us to talk in peace."

"This is my wife. Others may let you take charge, but don't even think of doing it to my wife." Michael stepped up beside her, covering the window. "I'll be back soon. Business is calling to me."

He kissed her lips once again. She didn't respond staying still. Holding her breath she waited for him to leave before turning back to Tate.

"Why did you let him kiss you?" Tate asked.

"He causes problems. I don't want to give him a reason to hurt you or the club."

"We're a family, Kels. He won't be getting to us. We're banding together to find out the truth about him." Tate stroked her head. "I was so fucking scared."

"I'm so sorry."

"You keep saying it. Stop. Why didn't you call me? I'll be there for you whenever you need me."

"I reacted, and I shouldn't." Kelsey pulled on her hand showing Tate what she meant. "I hate this. I'm trapped and can't get away."

"No talk of getting away. We'll all take care of you. Killer is handling everything."

Biting her lip, she looked at her best friend. "He's talking about having me moved from here to live with him."

"What? Live with Killer at the club? I've told him to start looking for a place to stay. There's no way you're staying at the clubhouse with all that shit going on. You're still a virgin, right?"

Her cheeks felt on fire. "Yes, I'm still a virgin. I'm not talking about Killer. This is all coming from Michael."

"He can't take you away."

"Not yet. I'm in too delicate a condition." Kelsey rolled her eyes. "He's feeding me now, too. I've spent more time in his company in the last day than I have in the entire time we've been married." She laughed then stopped feeling close to losing it.

"You're not alone anymore. Do you want me to call your family?"

"No, don't call them. They'll make everything worse. Please, promise me you won't call them."

Tate held her hands up. "I won't call them. Consider them off the list of people to call."

Relaxing, Kelsey closed her eyes trying to get her breathing under control.

"You lied about having the perfect family," Tate said.

"If you knew my parents you'd feel the same. No one needs to know a sorry sob story."

"I could hit you right now. We're friends, Kels. Best friends. I tell you about everything. Shit, we've almost died together. You mean far more to me than anyone else." Tate stood up, hugging her close.

Tears filled Kelsey's eyes at the emotion in Tate's voice. "I'm sorry."

"Stop saying that. We all love you, Kels. No more trying to kill yourself, do you hear?" Tate asked, glaring down at her.

"I've got the message loud and clear. I'd hug you, but I'm not allowed to. I'm being held back." She tried to make a joke, but it fell flat in the room.

"Sandy will take care of everything, honey. I'm going to try and get here more and more."

"What about Simon? He needs you."

"I'm devoting my time between the two. You're important to me, and I'd never forgive myself if I didn't divide my time. You were there for me when I needed you." Tate stood up, looking around. "This room sucks. I'm not surprised if you want to kill yourself. This room makes me want to commit suicide. It's so depressing."

Kelsey watched from the bed as she walked over to the window.

"It's too hot outside for you not to enjoy the fresh air." She pulled the chair along behind her, climbed up and opened the window.

The moment the window opened Kelsey felt the blast of warm air across her face. Closing her eyes she breathed out a sigh.

"How does that feel?" Tate asked.

"Perfect. It feels perfect. I love it."

"See, you're already smiling, and it has nothing to do with your fancy-pants husband. It's all down to me." Tate giggled. "Right, I think a television is needed or at the very least some books. Sandy will make sure you can hold them, but you've got to promise not to cause any more problems."

"I won't cause problems, Tate. I've learned my lesson."

Smiling, Kelsey watched her friend grow animated at making her life more comfortable.

The moment the door opened showing Michael the smile on her face dropped. He'd come to take her friend away.

"Your time is up."

Tate huffed, putting a hand on her hip. "I made her smile. I'm doing much better than you. What have you managed to accomplish? All you've done is make her feel sucky."

Michael didn't say anything. He stood waiting for her friend to leave. Tate blew out a breath. "Fine, fine, I'm going." She walked to the bed staring down at her. "I'll get everything changed to make your stay more comfortable. Don't let him get to you. We all love and miss you." Tate leaned down, kissing her cheek. "I'll tell

Killer how you're feeling."

"Please do."

She watched her friend go. When the door closed and Michael took a seat, Kelsey wished with all of her might she could get away from him.

Chapter Eight

Three days later

Killer waited in the hospital waiting room again. Tate had disappeared to go and see their woman. Michael was on the phone out in the parking lot. In the last three days they hadn't found anything else out about him. Alex was convinced by how little they found out about the financials that Michael wasn't all he seemed. He was staying out of Fort Wills at an expensive hotel, which was heavily guarded with a lot of muscle.

Some legit businessman wouldn't be keeping so many bodyguards. Alex's interest was piqued, and now he was determined to find out the truth about Michael.

Opening the latest woman's magazine, Killer lost interest the moment it started talking about what men really wanted. Couldn't women see each man was fucking different? There were men who loved thin, slender women while others liked a lot of curves, and others liked something in between.

He loved Kelsey's curves, her full tits and generous legs. Most of his nights were spent imagining her legs wrapped around his waist as he plowed inside her over and over again.

"It's a lovely day," Sandy said, taking a seat beside him. She wore a stethoscope around her neck, looking every inch the part of a professional doctor.

"Yeah, it is. So what? Can you sneak me inside while he's arguing on the phone?" Killer asked.

Sandy smiled. "I can do more than that, but I think you need to take a walk around the cafeteria garden. Have a coffee, relax and take in the sunshine."

She linked their arms and tugged him to his feet. "I don't want to leave. What if he tries to take her away?" He needed to be there to stop the bastard at every turn.

"Why don't you follow me, and I'll escort you where you have to be," Sandy said. "Besides, he can't move her. Kelsey's injuries are not good."

Killer followed her in the opposite direction of the room. He didn't argue or put up a fight. Sandy was doing everything she could to keep Kelsey close by. Michael had already talked with the doctor about transporting her to a different hospital.

"It's only a matter of time before he tries to move her," Sandy said.

"I know. We've got to get her out of here."

"I spoke with the doctor who runs the psych ward. She's not a massive risk. He believes she made a mistake, but there is still the risk that she's acting. His word is what is keeping her under our protection," Sandy said, talking to him in a whisper.

"What is the doctor wanting in return for his help?"

"Some money and the agreement we'll keep an eye on his son when he requests to join The Skulls. I took him to meet Tiny the night before last."

"Shit, is this going to be too hard to deal with?" Killer asked.

"Nothing is too hard to deal with. Listen to me, Killer. Tiny will do anything for his club. You're a Skull, and your woman is in danger. Trust us to work with you."

"Okay. I'll trust you."

Sandy paid for two coffees, and then they headed out to the grounds. He went to sit at the nearest available bench.

"No, not there. Follow me."

Killer didn't argue. He noticed the attention he

got for his leather cut. The women were pushing their chests out begging to be looked at.

Looking over Sandy's shoulder he saw the object of his desire. Sandy moved out of the way for him to crouch down in front of her. Kelsey was sitting in a wheelchair with a blanket over her legs. Her arms were bandaged up. Her hair was piled up on top of her head cascading around her face. Even in her hospital gown, she looked totally beautiful.

"Baby," he said, catching her cheeks and slamming his lips down on hers.

"Killer." She pressed her head against his. "Tate helped me escape. I'm not tied to my bed anymore." She lifted her arms up for him to see. "See, I'm all free."

"She's not allowed out of the wheelchair," Sandy said. "We'll leave you for a few minutes. Take her for a spin around the garden. It's a lovely place to sit around and enjoy." Sandy took Tate's arm leading her away.

Going behind her, Killer walked around the garden, staring down at his woman every now and again.

"How did this get worked out?" Killer asked. If Michael knew what was happening, he knew the other man would do everything in his power to stop what was happening.

"Michael left to deal with business. Something bad is happening, I don't know what. He's getting a lot of calls lately that make him look worried," Kelsey said. "When he was out of the room, Tate got the wheelchair, and Sandy went to get you." She looked behind her. "Are you happy to see me?"

Leaning down, he cupped her soft cheek, sliding his tongue into her mouth. "More than you can know." Closing his eyes, he let out a groan. "I'm rock hard for you right now."

She smiled. "I love you, too."

"Love you always. My love has nothing to do with what I want to do to you."

"I'm surprised you can think of that with these in the way." She touched each of her wrists in turn. Her face took a somber look to it.

"Hey, don't you think about that." He surrounded her hands where she held onto her wrists. "This is nothing. Do you hear me? Nothing."

Glancing around he saw they were gaining a lot of attention.

Wheeling her away from all the prying eyes, he found a secluded alcove that would give them the privacy they needed.

He tugged the blanket from her legs.

"Killer, I'm not allowed to be without it," she said.

"It's hot, baby. You don't need this blanket." He tugged her to her feet, wrapping his arms around her waist. Her curves molded to him. With her so close he forgot all about their troubles. The only two people who existed in the world were him and her. "It's boiling outside, and besides, no one can see us. We're all alone here. Hold me."

She banded her arms around his neck. He ignored the feel of her bandages against his neck.

"We shouldn't be doing this."

Reaching down to cup her ass, he gripped her tightly, lifting her up against him. She had no choice but to circle his waist with her glorious thighs.

"Killer," she said, moaning.

Pushing her against the hard brick, he pressed his rock hard erection to her core. "Do you feel me, baby? I fucking crave you." Nudging her head up to look at him with his nose, he claimed her lips devouring her mouth for his own pleasure.

She whimpered, thrusting against his cock.

"That's it, baby. I love you, and if we were away from here I'd make love to every inch of your body. I know it would be your first time, so I'd make every second feel fucking amazing for you."

Nibbling at her lips he waited for her to open before he slid his tongue into her mouth. "Killer, please," she said, begging.

"I know, baby." Putting her to her feet he pressed a hand to the front of her gown. He felt her quivering stomach. Going further down he cupped her between her thighs. "How do you feel? Do you want me to touch you?"

"Yes," she said, crying out. Lifting up the dress of her nightgown, he covered her body so anyone passing wouldn't suspect what he was doing. If he knew more about her condition he probably would hold off touching her, but Killer only saw their combined pleasure.

She wasn't wearing any panties. He slid his fingers through her creamy slit.

"Do you want me?" he asked.

"Yes."

"Tell me to finger your pussy."

Kelsey closed her eyes, shutting him out. He wouldn't let her hide from him. "Look at me, Kels. There is only you and me. Us together and I want to feel you come apart."

"Finger my pussy, Killer," she said.

Circling her clit he watched the rapture cross her face as she sank against the wall.

"Good girl. When we get away from here, Kels, I'm going to tongue your sweet pussy and bring you to orgasm many times. By the time I get my cock inside you, you'll be screaming for more." Tasting her lips he glided over her swollen clit. Her fingers sank into the hair at the nape of his neck.

She shook in his arms. He caught every moan that left her mouth.

"Come for me, baby."

Within seconds she shattered apart in his arms. Her eyes went wide as he continued to stroke her.

He stared down into her eyes as he brought his wet fingers to his lips to suck off her glorious cream. "Beautiful," he said.

After he got her together he helped her back into the wheelchair. "What about you?" she asked.

"I'm happy to have touched you."

****

The hard ridge of Killer's cock pressed against the front of his jeans. Kelsey wasn't blind and knew he must be in pain with a cock the size of his. Her whole body felt on fire from his touch.

Grabbing his neck she tugged him close needing his lips on hers. Their life in a matter of days had become so messed up. She didn't know what they were going to do. Tate, Sandy, and Killer each assured her they were working on handling Michael. Whatever plagued her so-called husband kept him away, which she was thankful for.

"I can help you." She whispered the words against his lips.

"Baby, I'm not having you take care of my dick in the hospital. Touching you now is more than I deserve." He stroked her cheek, smiling at her. "We'll have time for more. I promise."

"I wish we didn't have to have promises."

"Until Michael is out of our lives it's all we've got."

She looked down at her lap. He tucked the blanket back around her keeping her warm. The tender way he touched her always caught her by surprise. She never put gentle and Killer together in the same ring, but it was true. Besides the truth about his screwing another woman he'd never actually hurt her.

Still, even as she thought about the other woman she couldn't stop thinking about her *husband.* They'd both made a mistake. She could forgive and forget if he would be willing.

He tucked some loose strands behind her ear. "You're so beautiful."

Kelsey remained silent never knowing what to say to him when he spoke words of love and beauty.

"It's time for us to finish our stroll," he said.

She rested her head on her palm staring at people as they passed. The women were all looking at Killer. The lust shone in their eyes at the sight of him. She wanted to get up and smack them to stop them looking at her man.

The men stared at Killer with envy. They were clearly taken in by his tattoos and leather jacket. The Skulls were known far and wide.

"What the fuck are you doing here?" Michael asked, stepping forward.

Shit, he looked ready to do murder. Glancing behind her she saw Killer held the same look on his face.

"I'm taking her for a walk."

"You're not supposed to be here. When are you going to learn your fucking place?" Michael asked. His voice rose turning them into a spectacle.

"Michael, stop it," she said, wanting the ground to open up and swallow her.

"No, I let Tate in, but now I find you being taken out by this piece of shit."

She tensed. "Stop it!"

He charged behind her intent on pushing Killer

out of the way. Both men were large, and Kelsey wasn't interested in being the thorn between them. Spinning as far as she could, she pressed her palm on top of Killer's. "Take me back to my bedroom. I don't want any of you starting a fight. We're in the hospital gardens."

Gripping the blanket tighter she waited for them to start moving. Tate and Sandy were returning. When they saw what was going on, they charged their way.

"You're not seeing her again," Michael said, glaring at both women.

"You can't fucking stop me, asshole." Tate stepped right up to Michael. "You want to piss on her, go ahead. She's my best friend. She wanted to see Killer, and I, like the good friend I am, made sure she got what she wanted."

"You wanted to see Killer?" Michael asked, turning his gaze back to her.

"Yes."

Silence fell on the group. She tensed waiting for the inevitable argument. Why couldn't he see that she was in love with Killer?

No one spoke a word as Killer started moving. They made their way to her room. He picked her up easing her back on the bed.

"I can fucking do that—"

Michael didn't get to finish what he was saying before Killer had him locked up against the far wall with an arm across his neck. "Who the fuck do you think you are?" Killer asked, growling in the other man's face.

Kelsey panicked. "Stop it, the both of you, stop it."

Sandy and Tate tried to pull Killer off, but he wasn't having any of it.

"I'm sick to fucking death of you throwing your name around. She's mine, dammit, mine."

Security rushed through the room tearing Killer off. He was pulled out of the room, yelling at Michael. "I'll find the fucking truth out about you, fucker."

She glanced toward Michael to see him smiling smugly. He clearly wanted Killer to attack him, but why?

"Get out," he said, pointing a finger at Tate. "You'll be lucky to see her again soon."

Tate, always so stubborn, walked over to her. "I'll see you tomorrow, honey. Just wait and see if anyone can stop me." She kissed her cheek before leaving the room.

"I'll have a guard of my choosing posted at this door," Michael said, glaring at Sandy. "When the time is right, you're leaving this place."

Panicking, she glanced at Sandy, seeing the shock in the other woman's face. "You can't take her away. This is where she has to stay."

"No, I'm doing what I think is best for my wife, and it's not staying here with you fuckers. I don't want him near my woman."

"I'm not yours," Kelsey said, speaking up.

"You're mine. Your name is Kelsey Granito, and it's time you started using it."

He stared down at her. The glare he sent her way startled her enough to sit back on the bed. She felt torn between arguing with him or doing as she was ordered.

"Leave," he said, talking to Sandy. He didn't break eye contact but ordered Sandy out of the room.

For once the other woman didn't argue with an order.

She stared at the door closed shut behind her.

"Why?" she asked, staring back at him.

"Why what? I'm not a mind reader."

"Why do you care? You've been out of my life for so long. Why do you care *now*?" All the time they'd been together he never showed any point in caring about her. "None of this makes any sense. You live your life, and I live mine."

"It's going to change. There's no getting out of our contract, Kels. You've got to face facts. Your life belongs to me now."

She shook her head. "No, you're insane."

"I'm not. One day you'll see how much I'm protecting you. The moment the doctor signs off on your condition I'll move you. You'll have nothing to do with The Skulls."

This was the last thing she wanted.

"What about my mental state? I could try to kill myself again." She winced at the hysteria coming from her.

"You and I both know you're not going to try that again. No, you're fine, and I'm not letting you blind me into doing what you want." He buttoned up his jacket. "With Killer and the rest of those fucking bikers out of the way I can finish my business here."

He walked to the bed. She jumped out of the bed and glared at him. "What makes you think I'll even come with you? I'm not a child, Michael. You can't hold Santa over my head."

His smile taunted her. "I'm not going to hold Santa over your head. I'm simply going to tell you the truth. You try to put up a fight, and I'll make sure The Skulls are hit at every angle with the law, the banks, and anyone I can bring to my power to make their life difficult. Killer is a criminal, and I'll make sure he goes away for a very long time. It's easier than you realize to get people put away. All it takes is a little nudge and a lot of money, both of which I have."

The threat was clear. She jerked away from him when he made to kiss her.

"I can wait. It won't be long before you get used

to my touch," he said.

In the next instance he left the room. Sandy stood outside waiting. She saw the other woman, who looked concerned.

"You may go in. Be warned, this will be the last time you get to see her."

Sandy charged into the room, shutting the door behind her. "What the hell is going on?"

"He's posting a guard at my door. I won't be able to leave without him present. We messed up, Sandy. The moment the doctor signs me off he's taking me away."

"You're an adult, Kels. He can't do anything against your will," Sandy said, stroking her hair.

"He can. He's threatening Killer and all of the club. I can't let them be hurt because of me."

"Stop worrying. It's time someone worried about you for a change rather than the other way around. I'll talk with the others. Trust me, Kels. You won't be leaving here with anyone but Killer." Sandy kissed her head and walked out of the room.

Twenty minutes later a knock sounded at her door. A tall man similar to Killer in height opened the door. "I'm Ben, and I'll be on your door. I don't like stupid behavior, so do as you're told and we'll get on fine."

Kelsey hated him on sight. What the hell was she going to do?

****

Zero stared across the parking lot to watch Michael Granito enter an abandoned club on the outskirts of the city. For a reputable businessman he sure looked out of place in the seedy part of town. Zero had been dropped off by Nash, and he was camping out in a worn down car where no one suspected someone to be scoping the place. Killer had stormed into the clubhouse threatening to kill the asshole.

Tiny refused to give the order of taking a man out until they'd exhausted all of their contacts. Alex had travelled back to Vegas to get more hands on in the search for details.

Taking pictures, Zero was bored with staying outside of the warehouse when he could get closer. His orders were specific, get pictures but don't get caught. He preferred to live dangerously, but with Tiny's recent warning, Zero wasn't in the mood to get the hiding of his life.

Once again Tiny had pulled him aside because of Sophia. He'd also noticed that often when she entered a room and spotted him, she turned around and left. Zero hated what he was doing, but he couldn't stop it. Most of the time she left him alone, not speaking to him or moving away if he got too close. Shit, he needed to learn to stay away from the other woman. She was going to end up being the cause of him saying bye to life if he wasn't careful.

A few more pictures were taken. Four men were stood in a circle, smoking, laughing, and cheering as they spoke. He took a swig of his bottled water, waiting for what was going to happen next.

His boredom complete, he flicked open and closed his cell phone, wondering if he should call and check in with Prue. The other woman had been a lifesaver, and he owed her a lot more than the money he sent her way.

Clicking her number into the cell, he paused as the door slammed open. Glancing through the hole in the door he watched one big giant man come out gripping the hair of a young girl. He tensed as the men moved out of the giant's way.

"No, please, I just want to go home. No, please."

She was thrown to the ground. The big guy withdrew a gun, aimed, and then fired splattering the girl's brains all over the rubble.

"What the fuck?" one of the men asked.

"She's a bad investment. No bad investment makes it past the big man." The giant walked away closing the door behind him.

Heart pounding, Zero wondered what the fuck Kelsey had stumbled into. The girl was a sweet one, and he knew she wouldn't have done it on purpose, but still, they were all fucking dead if they didn't deal with this shit-fest.

Three hours later, sweat poured down Zero's back. The body had been dragged away, the section of blood-coated rubble removed.

There was no color in Michael's cheeks as he stared down at the ground. Zero frowned. What the fuck was going on?

Once they were all gone, he pulled his cell phone back out of his pocket, dialing the club's number.

"What do you have for me?" Tiny asked.

"Sir, I'm starting to think we're in some fucking drama program or novel. You're not going to believe the shit I've just seen."

Climbing out of the car, he told Tiny everything he saw.

"Shit, Nash is on his way. Come back and inform the others. Shit is about to hit the fan, and I want everyone close when it starts to hit back."

Closing his cell, Zero stared at the patch the girl had been. She didn't look a day older than fifteen. He was once reminded of another young girl he'd helped away from men intent on hurting her. Zero had promised her brother he'd take care of her.

He hoped he lived long enough to uphold his part

of the bargain.

Chapter Nine

"Fuck, I knew it. I knew the bastard was into something," Killer said, slamming his palm on the table. Since being kicked out of the hospital he'd been camping outside trying to find a weakness in the fucker guarding Kelsey's door. He couldn't believe Michael had put a guard on her door.

Sandy had already warned them all about what he planned to do with Kelsey when she got the all-clear from the doctor. There was only so much the doctor in control of the final decision could do before he let her go. All the club members were having a meeting with the hope of finding a solution to the problem. At the beginning of the conversation, Killer had had to convince all of the club that he wasn't angered by Kelsey's lies. He was more than happy to forgive if she was. The club didn't like her lies but were willing to move on if he was. The women along with the men were all in the room. The sweet-butts were nowhere to be seen. This was club business, and they didn't need the sweet-butts for this.

"He kills women?" Angel asked, looking pale.

Lash wrapped his arms around her. "I won't let anything happen to you, baby."

Watching the two filled Killer with envy. Out of all of the couples they had to be the sweetest. Angel was so out of place within the club, but Lash would not have any other woman by his side. Alex was on the speakerphone from Vegas.

"Tell me again what you saw, Zero," Alex asked.

Zero went over what happened from dragging the woman out of the warehouse to her being shot in the head. "He kills women."

"No, it's more complex than that. Killing women would have alerted the authorities to what was going on,"

Alex said. "My men are finding a lot of inconsistencies at the moment."

"Why don't you tell us what you've found," Tiny said.

"Okay, up until the death of Michael's father, he was living the jet-setting life. He organized board meetings and kept the legitimate business running. They made money, and no one looked toward the father. Michael screwed what he wanted and worked all hours."

Killer sat down, listening with dread of what was to come.

"Then the old man dies, and suddenly Michael becomes a recluse. He's no longer known to the world. No models, no limelight, and no photographers. It's like he ceased to exist," Alex said. "There are women he screws, but none of them will talk. They're all silent."

The sound of paperwork being ruffled came across the line. If anyone was to find the truth out about the fucker, it was Alex.

"We all know that's possible. Look what happened to Snitch," Murphy said, speaking up.

Glancing over at his friend, he watched Tate caress his arm. The anger on Murphy's face showed his emotion.

"He didn't disappear though. This is where the inconsistencies occur. It's so fucking obvious I'm surprised the law hasn't seen the pattern." Alex stopped speaking, and more papers were rustled. "Every city he visits a variety of girls go missing. Most of them from rough neighborhoods, so I'm guessing the ones who will not be missed. Blonde, brunette, redhead that sort of thing. My men are thorough, and they've matched the girls to the areas so far."

"Shit, Alex, how do you get men to do all the work so quickly?" Butch asked, smirking. "Do you give them a bit extra on the side?"

Rolling his eyes, Killer stared at the speakerphone with a desperate need to know more.

"I pay them. Anyway, Michael turns up to this area about a week after a select number of girls go missing. He stays for a few days and then leaves. The girls are never seen from. Oh, wait … ten girls have been seen in the last five years. They've been found dead. Most of them known as escorts or prostitutes."

"Wait a minute," Zero said, leaning forward. "You're telling me the cops find these missing girls but still don't want answers to what made them go missing as young girls?"

He saw the anger on Zero's face. Killer couldn't argue with the man. He was so fucking angry that anyone wanted to hurt a woman.

"I'm not saying it's right, Zero. These girls are from bad neighborhoods. The statistics speak for themselves. Most runaways turn to the life on the streets, and sex is the oldest profession in the books."

"Do we have confirmation about Granito's involvement? I'm not going to start accusing him to have him laugh in my fucking face," Killer said. "We need to have proper proof."

"I'm working on the proper proof. He's good, but everyone makes a mistake, Killer. I'll get to the bottom of it."

They all muttered their appreciation. Killer reluctantly agreed. They would be back to square one if it wasn't for Alex.

"Can I go now?" Alex asked.

"Not yet, we've got a problem," Tiny said, looking toward Sandy.

"In the next couple of weeks Kelsey is going to be well enough to be moved. Her stitches will come out soon, but the doctor needs to make sure the wounds are closing without infection," Sandy said.

"So?" Alex asked.

"Michael is threatening the club, Alex," Killer said, speaking up. "He threatened all of us and Kelsey. She's scared of making a wrong move in case he takes it out on the club."

"I hate this fucker."

"Agreed. I need to know if there is any way of getting her out of sight away from his prying without being seen." Killer already had a plan. It was just a question of implementing it.

"I've got the means of getting you out of the way. I just need a time, and I can get you the place," Alex said.

For the next ten minutes they organized the means of getting Kelsey out of harm's way. He didn't believe Michael would hurt her, but Killer refused to take that risk. Her life came first. Killer also wasn't prepared to let her go.

Alex hung up, leaving the room silent.

"With this new threat I want you all on lockdown," Tiny said.

The women started complaining. Tiny held his hand up, cupping Eva's cheek with the other. "It's not going to be a conventional lock in. You'll be staying in the club, and the sweet-butts will be sent to their own quarters. Whenever the women go anywhere I want them escorted by a full member along with a prospect. We've all got too much to lose nowadays. I'm not going to risk any chance of losing any of you."

In the last two years, The Skulls had buried a lot of people. Killer wished he could take away this new fight. If he could walk away from Kelsey he would, but she owned his heart and soul. She made him a better person.

"I knew you'd all have some complaints, but keep your shit together. If Eva and I are staying here then you lot can as well. No arguments unless you want your ass kicked." Tiny kissed Eva's lips.

The meeting came to a close. Tate walked up to him. "You're not going to let him take her, are you?" she asked.

"No, he's not taking Kelsey away from us."

She tapped his arm. "Thank you for everything."

"I'm not doing this for you. I'm doing this for me and for Kelsey."

"I don't care who you're doing it for. The fact is, you're doing it. I'm so sorry for being a bitch to you." She went on tiptoes and kissed his cheek. "Thank you."

He watched her pass, catching Murphy's eye. Coming from Tate, he knew this was going to be the best apology he'd get. "Be safe with this. We don't want to lose another man," Murphy said.

Thinking about Time, Killer nodded. He joined Zero and Whizz at the bar, ordering a scotch. His life was going to get very hectic in the next couple of days. Tonight he'd relax, have a few drinks before heading out. Steven was going to drive him.

Zero poured them all out a scotch. "Let's make a toast," he said.

Raising his glass, Killer stared at Zero. The other man looked distraught.

"To women, their problems, and their pussies, all of which draw us in and spit us back out again," Zero said, knocking back the scotch.

"Colorful toast," Whizz said, drinking his scotch.

Killer finished his drink off, waiting for another.

Glancing behind him, Killer saw Zero's problem. Sophia sat with her daughter on her lap. Nash had his arms wrapped around the back of her chair. He was glaring at Zero the whole time.

Too much drama for him.

Whizz wandered off, probably to go and do some digging on a computer somewhere.

"Go on, tell me how fucking insane I am," Zero said, taking another drink.

"She's another man's woman. Get over it."

"Like you're getting over Kelsey being Michael's wife? Surely you know what I'm fucking going through?" Zero stormed away from the bar, heading out. Following behind him, Killer kept his glass in his hand. The other man had taken the bottle of scotch. He found Zero leaning against the wall, drinking from the bottle.

"Give me some," Killer said, raising his glass.

"Fuck off, get your own."

"Are you even listening to yourself?" Killer asked, snatching the scotch from the other man's hand. "So she's taken. She's in love with Nash. You're never going to know what it's like to have her in your arms."

"Just like Kelsey is to you."

Shaking his head, Killer took a sip of the dark liquid. It was night, and the temperature had dropped slightly. He thought about Kelsey staring out of the window. She used to love cuddling up while looking out of the window.

"No, not like Kelsey and me. My woman is in love with me, Zero. She wants me, not Michael." Zero snorted. "Sophia dropped everything to help Nash. He was a drug addict and a fucking liability, and still when she could have chosen you, she stuck beside him."

Killer knew his words stung. If anyone had tried to say a similar thing to him, he'd have tried to take them out.

"You're loving this, aren't you?" Zero asked.

"You think I love stating cold harsh facts to a brother? No, you've got it wrong. I don't want to throw your feelings in your face. You're never going to be with that pussy. You've got to learn to see her that way."

Zero leaned against the brick building. "Fuck!" He shouted the word to the sky. "I've never been this fucking hung up over a woman."

"Are you sure it's over Sophia?"

"Yeah, I am."

Shrugging, Killer poured out another scotch. This would be his last drink for a long time. "You've got to think about everything you're going to lose. The club is everything, Zero. Don't throw it away on a pussy."

"She's more than just a pussy."

"Are you in love with her?" Killer asked.

"I don't fucking know."

"If you don't know the answer, then it's a no." Killer handed Zero the glass. He took it, swallowing down the liquid.

"This is bad news," Zero said. "I watched them pull that girl out of the warehouse, Killer. They didn't care. She was screaming, begging for her life. He took her gun out and shot her at point blank rage. It was a fucking mess."

"We'll stop it. We've got no choice but to stop him from hurting others," Killer said. He remembered the sick feeling the moment he saw Kelsey in the bathtub.

"I'm with you every step of the way," Zero said.

"I know." They clinked their drinks together. Looking up at the moon, Killer knew he didn't have a long time to get Kelsey away from Michael. The clock was ticking.

****

One week later

Earlier in the day Sandy had been by the club to tell him about the plans to move Kelsey out of the hospital. Michael had settled all the hospital fees and taken all the advisories for medical staff with him. All Sandy got the chance to hear was that he was taking Kelsey home away from all the problems that caused her to hurt herself. They didn't know all of Michael's properties. Killer wasn't going to risk Kelsey's life because he didn't act soon enough.

Gathering the necessary bags he handed them to Zero. The other man was coming with him tonight before returning to the rest of the group when they were done.

"Is this everything?" Zero asked.

"It's everything we need. Alex has arranged everything else."

"Good luck and try not to kill anyone." Zero shook his hand, and they parted outside of the clubhouse.

"Are you ready?" Steven asked.

"Yeah, you sure about this?" Killer climbed into the passenger side.

"With the clubhouse on lockdown I don't like screwing the sweet-butts with everyone around. The old ladies make me wish for one of my own."

"Any sign of Blaine and his family?" Killer asked.

"He's turning up tomorrow with Emily and Darcy. I hope we can get this shit settled in no time," Steven said. "I'm getting sick and tired of lockdowns."

Killer agreed, keeping his eyes on the road in front of him.

"Sandy is waiting for you. Try not to kill him," Steven said, dropping him off outside of the hospital. He caught sight of Stink, who was staying behind to grab Sandy.

"I'm not going to kill anyone."

"It's your woman, man. I wouldn't put it past you to kill in order to protect her."

Killer couldn't argue with that assessment. When it came to his woman, he'd kill anyone who tried to hurt her.

Getting out of the car, he slammed the door behind him. Kelsey didn't have a clue what was happening today. He hoped she didn't put up a fight.

Entering the hospital, he was wearing a sweater with a hood. For the next couple of weeks he was no longer Killer, a member of The Skulls. He was going to be Theodore Smith, kidnapper and a mechanic.

Sandy sat down looking through some paperwork. Taking a seat beside her, he tried to look like a man waiting for an explanation.

"Is everything in place?" Sandy asked.

"Yes, we've got no choice but to move tonight. Does she know?"

"No, I couldn't get to her. The bastard on the door takes his job way too seriously. I'm surprised he even leaves his post to take a piss. I keep looking for bottles filled with crap, he takes his job so seriously." Sandy placed her hand in his. "She doesn't have a clue what's happening. Give her this if she becomes a problem."

She withdrew her hand, and he saw the small syringe. "It will knock her out for about an hour."

Nodding, he stared into her eyes. "Thank you."

"I've done nothing really, Killer. Keep her safe. She did attempt to commit suicide."

"I will. You'll come out when we need you?" he asked.

"You can count on it. I doubt I'll have a job by the end of tonight." She wrapped her arms around him. "I'm going out to Stink. Good luck." She stood, leaving him alone.

Watching her leave the hospital, he stared down at the tiny syringe hoping he wouldn't need it.

Getting to his feet, he headed toward Kelsey's room. Without fail he saw the man guarding her door.

Stopping in front of him, Killer stared at him.

"What the fuck do you want?" the guard asked, glaring.

Dropping the hood, Killer stared at the man keeping him away from his woman. His anger was contained, but the thought of anyone hurting his woman or keeping him away from her, angered him.

"You?"

Smiling, Killer caught the other man around the throat, drawing him up the wall. He'd gotten his name for a reason. Michael Granito and all of their enemies needed to remember who he actually was. He didn't take shit, and anyone who crossed him faced death.

Leaning forward, he whispered against the other man's ear. "Tell Michael he should learn not to mess with me. I'm not some fucking thug. I will kill to get what I want."

The man struggled to little effect. No one was passing in the hallway. After a minute his eyes started to droop, and he was getting ready to pass out.

When the guard was out of it, Killer left him on the chair and entered her room.

She was curled up facing toward him. Her eyes were closed. Flicking on the light, he walked to her.

"Kelsey," he said, shaking her. She moaned, opening her eyes.

"What? What's going on?" she asked. Some rattling caught his attention. Around one of her wrists was a steel handcuff locking her to the bed.

"Who did this?" He touched the cold steel

wanting to hurt someone.

"The guard. He doesn't trust me. I tried to escape the night before last. Since then he's been chaining me to the bed whenever Michael leaves for the night." She sat up the best way she could. "Killer, what are you doing here? If Michael sees you he's going to hurt you and the club."

"Fucker is not going to do anything."

"No, I'm serious," she said, touching his hand as he made to leave the room.

"Listen, Kels. You've got two choices. You either go with me willingly, or I give you this," he said, showing her the syringe. "Your choice."

"I can't."

Leaning in close, he claimed her lips. "This is not a discussion. We're going. Which way do you chose we leave?"

She licked her lips. "Not that way," she said, pointing to the syringe.

"Good." Leaving her side, he went to the man sat in the chair. Sticking the needle into his arm, he plunged it down. "Sleep tight." Searching in the man's pockets, he fished out the key that was locking his woman away from him. Entering the room, he inserted the key, twisted and watched the cuffs spring free.

He cursed as she rubbed her wrist. There was a large strip of tape down her arm. Sandy told him she healed quickly but would need her dressings changed regularly. She had sorted out pain medication in case Kelsey needed it.

When he picked Kelsey up in his arms, she let out a little yelp. "What are you doing?" she asked. "Put me down. I can walk."

"No, I'm carrying you out of here. I don't have any shoes for you to wear. I've got no choice." Picking her up in his arms, he left the room not even glancing back.

"This is completely insane."

"I'm your captor, baby."

"What?" she asked, holding onto his neck.

"I'm kidnapping you. Do you like it?"

She chuckled. "You're insane."

"And you're a married woman. I feel we'll create a scandal together. It should be a lot of fun. Are you game?" he asked.

One of the women on the desk tried to stop them. "Security!" The woman shouted. Picking up his speed, Killer made his way outside. Steven was waiting in the parking lot with the lights turned off. He heard the noise of some security officers heading their way. Quickly securing Kelsey in the car, he turned around and landed the first blow to one officer. The second officer he punched in the gut before kicking out and taking his leg.

The third one got hit in the jaw. Climbing into the passenger side, he put the seatbelt on as Steven peeled out of the parking lot.

His heart was racing, but he didn't care. Kelsey was safe, and he'd gotten her out of Michael's clutches.

Whatever was to come, he'd handle.

****

The following morning Michael stood in his wife's empty room. The steel cuffs were dangling down the outside of the bed. His anger was acute. The man he'd posted on the door was only supposed to keep that fucking doctor and the Skulls out. Instead of listening to his instructions the man had stopped his wife from leaving her room. He'd probably made her more terrified of him. The staff was offering their apologies to him. He didn't need to listen to another man or woman tell him how sorry they were. There was only one doctor he wished to see, and for some miraculous reason, she wasn't in work today. He wasn't a fucking idiot, and he knew what was going on.

The Skulls had found some way to take his woman.

"I'm sorry, sir."

Glaring at the other man, Michael paced up and down the room. He didn't need her identity getting out or the fact she'd escaped him. Fuck, everything was turning to shit. When the family lawyer had taken him into his father's old office a few weeks after his death, he never expected this kind of shit. He wasn't a fucking criminal, yet he'd been dragged down through hell and back to try to make everything work.

"Who else knows about Kelsey?" He'd put this man on the door because of his fucking discretion. Everyone knew he was married, but no one actually knew who he was married to. Some of the women he fucked over the years and been seen with had turned up dead. He wasn't going to risk Kelsey's life.

"I informed the whole team, sir."

"What?"

"The whole security team is aware of her disappearance and is doing everything they can to bring her back."

Michael had never wanted to kill anyone at all in his whole life until that one moment.

"Are you fucking insane?" He caught the other man by the shirt, slamming him against the wall. "If anyone finds out where Kelsey went she'll be fucking dead. They've been plotting and scheming for years to bring me down after my father gave me this fuck up of a business. Do you really think she's safe with every fucker looking for her?"

He'd rather her run away and never return than

risk the kind of life his enemies would seek for her.

If I ever get the chance, I'm going to kill you, Father, over and over again.

A knock at the door sounded. Pulling away from the other man, Michael turned to face the head security. The man had a broken nose and looked particularly weary.

The news of Killer's involvement didn't surprise him. All Michael hoped for was he got to them before his enemies did.

Chapter Ten

Steven stopped the car about two hours from picking them up at the hospital. Killer shook hands with the other man before picking Kelsey up from the backseat. She'd been sleeping for the last hour, and he couldn't bring himself to wake her up. Zero was sitting in another car further up the road waiting to take them to their destination.

"What's happening?" Kelsey asked, waking up in his arms.

Zero climbed out, opening the passenger door. He eased her inside.

"Go back to sleep, baby. We'll be there soon enough."

"This is all very covert," Zero said, getting back behind the wheel.

"We know too much. She's in danger if she goes with him." Killer settled into the front passenger seat. He turned to watch his woman sleep peacefully.

"This is still fucking dangerous. You're going away without any of The Skulls surrounding you. How do you think you're going to fare any better?"

Rubbing a hand down his face, Killer was so fucking tired from all the fighting. When they got to the place Alex set up for him, he was going to sleep for a whole week.

"One raid on the clubhouse will see Kelsey in his hands. We can't hide her in the same town as The Skulls. This is the only way."

"I think you should have gotten in touch with Devil. He'd have taken you in."

Devil was the leader of Chaos Bleeds who'd settled in a town quite away from Fort Wills known as Piston County. Devil was close with Tiny and hadn't made it up to Fort Wills recently.

"I don't want her surrounded by another club. They've got their own business to deal with. I'm tired of them being part of ours," he said. He also didn't want any of the other men looking at his woman. The Chaos Bleeds crew was dangerous, far more dangerous than The Skulls. They followed their own set of rules that didn't always go with the Skulls' own.

"You're just jealous in case one of them catches Kelsey's eye," Zero said, laughing.

"How can you laugh at a time like this?"

"Stop being a pussy, Killer. We're on the road, and you've got to learn to lighten up. If you're constantly growling at people you're going to stick out like a sore thumb. You're no longer a Skull now. You're Theodore Smith, mechanic and living with your wife."

Glancing back to Kelsey, Killer felt his whole body relax at the sight of her. He'd do whatever it took to keep her safe by his side.

"Why don't you come with me?" Killer asked.

"Why would I do that?"

"Get away from Sophia, clear your head. Get your shit together."

Zero kept his gaze on the road ahead. "I might drop by, but I'm not staying around. Alex is going to meet us with everything you need."

For the next hour they drove in silence, neither of them needing to talk. Being part of a club they were more than used to dealing with late nights.

"Alex is up ahead."

Killer tensed up seeing two cars right up ahead. When Zero stopped the car, he climbed out, reaching in to shake Zero's hand. "Take care, man," Killer said.

"Keep safe, and remember, stay in touch."

He picked Kelsey up. She woke up as he was

resting her in the other car.

"Shh, I'm going to talk everything through with Alex. Stay here." He closed the door turning to Alex.

"This is a high risk, you know that right?"

"Yeah, I know. I've got to protect my woman."

"Okay. Here are your passports and new identities. You're a married couple and are settling down in a quaint little town. You can't wear your leather cut," Alex said, warning him.

"I left it back at the club. This is all I've got," Killer said.

"Right." Alex popped the trunk of the car. "Here are your cases. The house is fully furnished, and here are the keys. I've talked with the local man who owns the mechanic shop, and he's more than happy to have you around to take some of the workload off him."

Staring at the bags, Killer nodded. "You thought of everything."

"Got no choice. Here, take these and be careful. You get any trouble, don't hesitate to give us a call."

Shaking hands with Alex, Killer left him alone to climb behind the wheel.

"What's going on?" Kelsey asked.

"I'll tell you everything when we get there."

She stayed silent. Killer needed to think, and the only way to do that was on the road.

"Climb into the front," he said, slowing the car down. He could bear silence no longer.

Kelsey got into the front, doing her seatbelt up before glancing at him. He took hold of her hand, squeezing her.

"Don't worry about a thing. We're going to get through this together." He pulled away managing the roads.

"Where are we going?" she asked.

"Paradise Rocks. It's a small town. We've got a few members of The Skulls who live here. They're not fully fledged members, but they're a distant part of the club." Killer checked the address and entered the small town. The town center had a variety of shops including a diner, mechanic shop, and a small shopping mall along the end of the road. He spotted a sex shop along with many different shops. Exiting the town, he navigated the roads coming to a stop at a small home at the end of a long street. The house didn't stand out at all. In fact it looked like the twenty other houses along the strip of the road. He spotted the light on in the front window.

Climbing out, he waited for the door to open.

Seconds later a man with sandy colored hair appeared in the doorway. "You Theodore?"

"Yeah, are you Mason Terry?"

"Yep."

They shook hands pulling each other in to slap a hand on the back. "I've got bags in the back."

Mason moved to the back as Kelsey stepped out of the car. "Nice to meet you, sweetheart."

She nodded, looking toward Killer.

"He's good. He's one of us."

"Yeah, you'll be starting work on Monday. I've got everything set up for you."

Within twenty minutes Mason got him up to date, and they were alone in their house. Staring around the sitting room, he turned to look at Kelsey. She still wore her hospital gown and the band around her wrist. Heading into the kitchen, he moved back to her with a pair of scissors.

"What are you doing?" she asked, taking a step back.

"Now I know you're not going to kill yourself." He grabbed her wrist and slid the blade of the scissors across her skin. Snapping the steel blades closed, he removed her name. "We need to burn this."

"Yes, burn it. I don't want to have any memory of what I did."

He still held onto her hand. "You're always going to have a memory of what you did." Caressing the white bandage he stared into her eyes. "You'll always have your scars."

"I know."

"Oh, I need you to wear these." He pulled the rings out of his pocket.

"Wedding rings?"

"Yeah, until we've got some way of dealing with Michael with proof, we're staying out of sight." He slid the rings onto her finger and leaned down to kiss her hand.

"Thank you."

Tears were shining in her eyes when he pulled away. "I love you, Kels. I'll do anything for you."

She wrapped her hand around his neck and pulled him in close. "I don't deserve you at all."

"Ditto, baby."

He claimed her lips feeling complete once again. Holding her close, he squeezed her ass loving her plump flesh filling his hands.

Their moans mingled together.

They were interrupted by the shrill of the telephone.

"Fuck, they've got the worst possible timing," he said.

"I'm going to head for a shower." She moved away from him.

"No, you need a bath. Sandy told me you're not allowed to get them wet."

She nodded, showing her agreement before

leaving him alone.

"We're here," he said, answering the call.

"Good. Call if you get any more news," Tiny said.

"Has Alex got anything?"

"Nothing concrete. He will. You're just going to have to give him time. We'll get this fucker in no time."

"Mason Terry, is he a good man?" Killer asked. He needed to know who he could trust.

"Yeah, he's a good man. Doesn't come to Fort Wills often. Grew up moving from place to place. Last I heard he liked Paradise Rocks enough to settle down." Tiny gave him the details of the man staying in the same town as he was. "I'll call with more updates when they become available."

Killer said his goodbyes and hung up the phone.

Locking all the doors and windows he turned the lights off before heading upstairs with their bags. Leaving them in the bedroom he entered the bathroom. For a second the image of Kelsey lying surrounded in red water swam across his mind. He shoved the horrid image away.

He found her sat in the bath with her arms resting on either side. She turned to look at him as he entered.

Tears glistened in her eyes.

"Baby, what's the matter?" he asked, going to his knees by the bathtub.

"I can't wash myself. I can't get them wet. This is a nightmare." She wiped at her nose looking ready to bleat harder.

Removing his watch, he placed it on the sink. He took his time ridding himself of his clothing.

"What are you doing?" she asked, looking up his body.

His cock twitched, but he nudged her forward.

"I'm getting in the bath with you. I'll keep you nice and clean, baby." His cock, with a mind of its own, made its presence known. Nothing he could do would stop the arousal crashing over him.

Trying to be good, he pushed her cherry blonde hair off her shoulder, exposing the length of her neck. She shivered, and glancing down her body he saw her beaded nipples. Shit, she was as turned on as he was.

****

Kelsey didn't know what was happening to her. No man had seen her naked before. Had Killer seen her naked when he saved her from herself? He had to have. She'd been completely naked with nothing between them to keep her safe.

All the time they'd been together they hadn't been naked in each other's company. Now they were alone, naked in a bath. She felt the hard ridge of his cock against her back. His hands pushed the hair off her neck. Closing her eyes she bit her lip as his kissed her neck.

Her nipples tightened, and her pussy pulsed awakening once again for him.

"Killer," she said, moaning.

"I know, baby." He reached around stroking her neck.

Her pulse pounded against her skin. He had to feel it against his fingers.

"Kelsey," he said, nibbling on her neck.

Resting against him, she felt whole. Like the whole mess they'd been in was in fact a fantasy or bad dream while this was the truth.

"I love you," she said.

Down his fingers went to circle her nipples. Arching up, she wanted his touch to be harder.

"You drive me crazy when you say that."

Within seconds, he pulled away, removing his

hands from her body. "No, we can't do this tonight," he said.

Turning around to stare into his eyes, she frowned. "Why can't we do this?" she asked.

"I've just kidnapped you from the hospital. You've got bandages on your inner wrists, Kels. I'm not going to fuck you for the first time tonight or in the bath."

He gripped her arm, turning her back toward him. "We can."

"No, don't argue with me. You're not ready to take my cock, and I'm not about to feel guilty for what I want to do to you."

She watched him hold the sponge and start to soap her body. Kelsey wanted to argue with him. He was being unfair. Kelsey trusted him to help her get out of her marriage with Michael. Her marriage was only on paper. Neither she nor Michael had any feelings for each other. Killer was the man she wanted. She was ready to have sex with him.

Really? You're ready to fuck Killer?

Pausing she felt his touch all over her body. Did she want to have sex out of need or just so her first time was with him?

Her love for Killer was absolute, but with the presence of Michael, she had started to doubt their ability to stay together.

"I see you're thinking about what I've said." He kissed her temple before washing her hair. She stayed still even as he washed himself. When they were finished, he climbed out.

His cock stood straight out and rock hard.

She kept her gaze on his shaft, watching the tip leak his pre-cum out of the tiny slit.

"You're turned on," she said, pointing at his cock,

accusing him almost.

He chuckled. "I told you we were not having sex tonight. I didn't say anything about how much I want to be inside your tight pussy."

His words made her cheeks feel red hot to the touch.

"We can do something tonight. I'm ready."

Killer cupped her cheek, pressing his head to hers. "No, you're not ready at all. You will be, and when you are, there will be no stopping me."

She watched him hold a towel out for her.

"Come on, baby. It's time to rest." She stood up stepping into the towel he held out to her.

As she followed him to the bedroom, he dried his hair with a towel before running it over his body.

His body was to die for. Hard muscle covered in ink. She'd always gotten aroused by the sight of him without a shirt, and now she knew what he looked like completely naked. He bent down over the cases, opening each one.

"Here, I imagine you'll want to put this on to sleep in."

Catching the sheer nightwear she turned her back to him to dry her body. By the time she'd put the lace on she wondered what the point was. Anyone with good eyesight would see everything she had on offer.

Killer already lay in bed, staring at her. "Remind me to thank Alex when I see him next."

"Why?" she asked.

"That," he said, pointing at her body, "is fucking perfect." He lifted the covers giving her room to slide in.

"We're sleeping together?"

"We're married. Where else do you expect me to sleep?"

"Right." She toyed with the rings on her wedding

finger wondering how she was going to keep up the falseness.

Sliding under the covers, Killer banded an arm around her waist, drawing her close. She felt his cock rest against her ass.

"You're not wearing any clothes," she said.

"Of course not. I never wear anything to bed." He snuggled in close, his large body making her feel small compared to him. "One day you'll be wearing nothing at all."

"Why would I do that?" she asked, feeling wide awake.

"Through the night, I get horny. When you're naked I can slide into your body rather than take care of business with my hand. You'll come in handy." He kissed her neck, moaning.

Nipples hardening once again, she pressed her thighs together at the sudden heat swamping her core.

"You're wet right now, aren't you, baby?" he asked.

His lips were making her nerves stand on end.

"Yes," she said.

His fingers caressed her stomach before sliding down to cup her pussy. "Fuck, you're burning up." He pushed her nightgown out of the way to slide a finger between her wet folds. "Fuck." Killer kept cursing. "Why didn't you tell me how desperate you were?"

"I thought I did when I offered to sleep with you," she said, staring at the far wall.

The hard brand of his cock made it hard for her to focus on anything else but his touch. She felt on fire from it.

"We're not going to fuck tonight, baby. I'll take care of you," he said.

His other hand cupped her breast as he worked

her clit. She frowned. Killer was going to touch her bring her to another orgasm while she didn't even get to touch him?

No, she didn't want that.

Pulling out of his arms, she fell to her knees beside the bed.

"Fuck, Kels, what are you doing?" he asked, sitting up.

Getting to her feet, she glared at him, tucking some of her damp strands behind her ear. "I'm not doing it. I know I fucked up with these stupid scars, but I'm not going to live with it for the rest of my life." Tears filled her eyes once again, and she batted them away. She had fucked up. Cutting her wrists was the worst thing she'd ever done in her life and one thing she'd never repeat again. Glaring down at the man she loved, she waited for him to respond.

"What the fuck are you talking about?" he asked, climbing over the bed to stand in front of her.

She wasn't expecting that. Kelsey hoped he'd stay over his side keeping the bed between them.

"I made a mistake, and you're punishing me for it. In fact, I've made two mistakes."

"Tell me about these mistakes?" he asked, folding his arms over his chest.

"The first was marrying Michael. If I didn't agree to it then we wouldn't be in the position, and the second was trying to escape what I got caught up in." She held her wrist up showing the white strip across her scar.

Killer caught her wrist before she could pull away. Laying a kiss to her wrist, he stared into her eyes. "First, I wasn't with you when you were forced to either marry Michael or be turned out on the street. I hate the fact you married the bastard, but I can't regret you marrying him, Kels, especially knowing it led you to me.

You didn't stay at home and moved away. We're here now, in this together." His other hand sank into her hair, drawing her close. "I could fucking spank you for cutting your wrists. It's one of the most selfish acts I've known you to do."

She gasped, seeing the hurt in his eyes.

"I want to make something clear, Kels. I love you with all my heart and fucking soul, but if you ever try to take your own life again, I want you to know that I'll be fucking following you."

His words made her freeze. "What? You can't do that."

Killer pressed a finger over her lips. "Shut the fuck up. You've talked enough. It's time for me to have my say." He kissed her lips, resting his head against hers. "I can't imagine a life without you in it, Kels. You take your own life there is nothing left for me here. I've got The Skulls, but they'll never replace you. I'll take my own life to be with you."

Tears fell down her face. The conversation dulled any kind of arousal she had. "No, you can't do that. It's not fair."

"But you taking your own life was?"

"It was different."

"No, it wasn't any different. The next time you even think of ending your life I want you to remember this conversation."

He slammed his lips down on hers, plundering his tongue into her mouth.

Kelsey kissed him back knowing there was nothing more for her to say. She couldn't bear being the cause of taking Killer's life. Hating what she had done, Kelsey held onto him.

"Now, we're going to bed to sleep," he said, lifting her in his arms and drawing her back to bed.

This time she settled down without any argument. Killer wrapped his arms around her waist holding her in place.

****

Zero returned to the clubhouse later that night. Everyone was in bed, and he headed to the kitchen to grab a beer. Killer's offer had been fucking appealing, but Fort Wills was his home. There was no way he'd be leaving his home because he couldn't get his feelings under control over a fucking woman. He was better than that.

Popping open the cool beer he took a long swallow.

He needed to get his thoughts under control before he lost his mind over Sophia. She wasn't anything special at all apart from the fact she'd been the one woman he wanted and couldn't have. Yes, Angel was a beauty, and so were Tate and Eva, but there was something different about Sophia.

Fuck, Nash should be his main priority as he was a Skull, his brother. He shouldn't be having these feelings for Nash's woman. Swallowing down more of the alcohol he stared up at the ceiling praying for some kind of sign to get him over her.

"Oh, you're back," Sophia said, appearing in the doorway.

Give me a fucking break already.

"Yeah, I just got in." He moved away from the fridge, brushing past her as she walked to it.

"How are Kelsey and Killer?" she asked.

"Fine, last time I checked they got there safely and we've got nothing to worry about." He tipped the bottle back, swigging more of the beer down.

"Good, I'm glad. I was worried about you all." She pulled out a bottle, and he watched her place it in the microwave.

"Is she up?" he asked, referring to her daughter.

"Yeah, Nash is calming her down while I get the bottle." She tested the bottle then turned back to him. "Are you all right?"

Zero watched her lean against the fridge. Her dark hair spread out around her. She wore one of Nash's shirts, which came to her knees. Instead of thinking she looked a mess, he got turned on by the sight of her alone.

Closing the distance between them, he sank his fingers into her hair. She gasped, eyes widening as she stared up at him.

"What are you doing?" she asked.

Her hand pressed on his chest. Leaning down he was a breath away from her lips.

Don't do this. A line will be crossed.

Gritting his teeth, he forced himself to pull away. "Fuck!" Slamming his fist against the fridge, he took a step away. "Stay the fuck away from me."

He stormed out of the room ignoring the shock and fear reflected in her eyes. Zero knew he needed to get his shit together before he ruined his position within the club.

Chapter Eleven

Killer heard Kelsey in the kitchen. From the sheer nightgown lying in the laundry basket he knew she was fully dressed. Rubbing the sleep from his eyes he glanced around the room wishing he'd woken to her in his arms. The scent of coffee wafted up to him. Climbing out of bed, he did his business and turned the shower on. He needed to wake up fully. Being sleepy was not going to do for the rest of the day.

Stretching the sleep out of his body, he turned the shower on waiting for the water to warm up. Since the night of Kelsey's attempted suicide he'd not slept well at all. He'd not been lying last night either. There was no reason for him to keep on living if he didn't have his woman. Letting the warm water cascade down his body, he fisted his length feeling the arousal start to stir.

Thinking about Kelsey in the sheer nightwear he moaned, resting his head on his arm as he worked his arousal. If she'd not pulled away last night he'd have been tempted to fuck her. There was only so much a man could take before he gave in to temptation and took what he wanted. The imagined feel of her tight cunt brought him to orgasm quickly. He gritted his teeth keeping the noise locked inside.

The orgasm was nice but not what he really craved. Watching the white strands of his semen wash down the drain, he finished in the shower. Once out, he dried and dressed himself quickly. The scent of bacon mingled with the coffee, calling to him.

Heading downstairs, he placed a shirt over his head, rounding the corner to find Kelsey standing in a pair of jeans and shirt.

She turned to smile at him. The shirt was long enough to hide the bandages on her arms. Sandy had told him she'd need to change them this morning and had talked him through what he needed to do.

"Morning," she said.

"Morning." He walked to her, landing a kiss on her head before taking a seat. Looking down at his hand he stared at the gold band on his wedding ring. Fuck, he was starting to feel like a fucking pussy. Killer wanted to bind Kelsey to him giving her no choice but to stay with him.

He wished their marriage was fucking real. Fisting his hands, he thought about Michael wondering what the bastard was thinking right that second.

"Did you sleep well?" he asked.

"Yeah, I hope you don't mind. I started making some breakfast for us both," she said, handing him a coffee.

Grabbing her hand, he tugged her close after she'd put the steaming mug in front of him. "I missed you." She rested on his lap with her hands gripping his shoulders.

"I wanted to make you something," she said. Her gaze dropped to his lips. Cock filling back up, he claimed her lips, sliding his tongue inside her mouth.

She pulled away first. "The bacon will burn."

Releasing her, he let her go to finish breakfast. Sipping his coffee, he watched her move around the kitchen. Her ass was so fucking full, begging to be spanked. He couldn't wait to get her ready to sink inside her tight flesh.

"This is our house now, Kels. You've got to get used to working inside it," he said, taking another sip of coffee.

"I know. It's just weird." She served up their breakfast, moving to sit beside him. The shirt she wore was tight around her breasts, showcasing the full mounds.

One day he'd have her naked at his table while they ate.

"We've got to make the most of our situation." Picking up his knife and fork he dived into the eggs and bacon.

"Killer, I don't regret us sharing a house. What I hate is knowing it'll come to an end," she said, smiling sadly at him.

Grabbing her hand, he stared into her eyes. "When all this is over we'll find a place together."

"When all this is over I won't have the money."

"You're a dental nurse, Kels, and believe it or not, I've got quite a bit put by for a rainy day."

She chuckled, and he loved the sound.

They ate their breakfast in silence. Killer placed his cell phone on the table in case of any incoming calls. He wasn't in a rush to end their time together, but he wanted Michael out of their life.

"What do you think we should do today?" she asked, standing up.

"I'll help you with the dishes." He dried all the dishes loving the domestic feeling of being stood by her in their home.

Not our home.

The moment the danger was all over, he'd be investing in their own place.

"We're going out. I'm going to get myself acquainted with the new boss, and we're going to be seen around town."

"Where is your leather cut?" she asked.

"Keeping a low profile, baby. No cut and no mention of The Skulls. We're a married couple trying to make a life for each other."

She finished washing the sides down as he went

back to grab the bag Sandy packed for him. Sitting at the table he changed her dressings checking over her marks before covering them back up.

"Thank you," she said.

"No need to thank me. Come on, let's get out of here."

Together they left the house, climbing into the car to head back into town. He found an available parking space in the parking lot around the back of the small shopping mall.

He took her hand, and they headed out together. He nodded at people they passed. Wearing a long shirt covered up his tats. For the first time since he joined The Lions, he was finally a civilian. Women still gazed his way. A few men stared at Kelsey, but she clung to his side like a lifeline. Compared to the women she looked pale. She'd not gotten out all that much to get some sun.

With them being alone away from the danger he'd make sure she spent a great deal of time in the garden getting a tan.

"Do you think we'll fit in?" she asked.

"We're already fitting in." Crossing the main road he headed toward the mechanic shop where Mason stood waiting.

"Hey, man. I didn't think you'd make it in today."

"Wanted to come and meet the man I'm working for," he said.

The shop had two cars already in place to be worked on underneath.

"Jason is in his office. Be careful. He's not in a good mood, but then, he's rarely in a good mood," Mason said.

Leaving Kelsey with the other man he made his way toward the back. Knocking on the partially open door Killer waited for permission to enter the room.

"What?" The harsh voice called through.

Entering the room he stared at the middle aged man behind the desk. His head was bent over a sheet of numbers. His temples were graying, and Killer spotted ink up and down the man's arms.

"Are you the fucker Alex wants to put to work?" Jason asked, looking up. There was a scar down one side of his face. He looked vicious, scary, and not altogether pleasant.

"I guess so." He took a seat in the chair opposite. "Last I checked Alex is paying you to pay me."

"Yeah, I owe the fucker my life." Jason pointed to his eye. "Can you at least work on cars? Last thing I need is for you to fuck up the cars we've already got in place."

"Yeah, I can work on cars."

"Good, that's all I need to know. You're starting on Monday. I don't want any bad shit brought to my establishment. I hear you got a woman with you?"

"Yeah, she's out front with Mason. You want me to introduce her?"

Jason nodded. "I want to see if she'll cause me any trouble."

Leaving the office he found Kelsey stood along the far wall watching Mason work on the car. "Hey, baby." He tugged her close, slamming his lips down on hers. She moaned, opening up to him. "Kelsey, I'd like you to meet my new boss, Jason." Killer introduced the two.

"It's so good of you to take him," she said, offering her hand.

"Are you satisfied?" Killer asked.

"Yeah, for now. Come back on Monday. You'll have work waiting for you then." Jason walked away.

Mason cleaned his hands on a towel moving toward them. "He's moody but a good boss. You won't be disappointed."

Killer wouldn't dispute that. Taking Kelsey around the town he felt himself begin to relax. The outside world could wait. For now, it was just him and Kelsey with their troubles being handled by the rest of the club. He wasn't going to waste a single moment of it.

****

Slamming the door of his car, Michael buttoned up his shirt and entered The Skulls' domain. Cars and bikes filled the compound, and the mechanic shop was closed for a change. He didn't enter Fort Wills without being completely in the know about The Skulls.

They caused a problem for anyone who entered their territory about to break the law.

"What the fuck are you doing on my land?" Tiny said, coming out of the door. Several men and a couple of women exited the clubhouse to face him.

Michael knew all of their names, including the women. He spotted Angel instantly. One of his men thought she'd pull in a tidy sum, but there was no way any of them was willing to take on Lash. Nasty business dealing with the biker group, not to mention their connection to Chaos Bleeds, which kept most of their enemies away.

He noted Killer was missing from the group. "Where is she?" he asked.

"Who?" Zero asked.

"You can play games all you want. Kelsey is mine. It won't be long before I get her back and Killer is in prison for kidnapping."

The threat was not an empty one. He imagined his own enemies were already on the hunt to use her against him. Fuck, this was becoming more of a mess than he anticipated. Maybe he should have divorced her when she asked. What was the point in staying married to a woman who clearly didn't want him?

Sandy stood glaring at him with hands on her hips.

"Do you really think this is clever keeping her away from me?"

"Kelsey wants a divorce. You ever thought she might take matters into her own hands," Tate said, speaking up. Murphy had his hands on her shoulders keeping her back.

Tiny stared back at him, looking him up and down.

"Get inside," Tiny said, to all of them.

Michael watched as all of Tiny's people left him alone. "That was a bit stupid, don't you think?"

"You're nothing but a boy playing in a tank full of sharks. Your first mistake was coming into my town."

"What's my second?" Michael asked.

"Thinking we wouldn't find out the truth." Tiny closed the distance between them. When he placed his hands on Michael's shoulders it took all of his strength not to crumble under the pressure. Tiny was an older man, but he sure wasn't weak.

Tiny smirked, clearly seeing how strong he was. He fisted the lapels of his jacket. Michael jerked in his arms feeling more like a rag doll than a fully grown man.

"Michael Granito, Fort Wills is my town, and I take care of everyone in my town."

"What the fuck are you getting at?" Michael asked, gritting the words between his teeth.

"What am I getting at?" Tiny asked, smiling.

Nodding, he glanced behind him knowing his guards were waiting for the signal to come to his aid. The last thing he needed was for this man to see him in need of help.

"I know about you. I know about the girls. If I so much as find any of our women, and I don't just mean the club women, missing, I'm coming for you. All of my enemies have one destination. Do you know where?"

Michael waited for Tiny to finish.

"In the ground. Fuck with me and it will be your last act." Tiny shoved him away. "Get the fuck off my property."

****

One week later

Kelsey checked over the chicken with garlic and thyme in the oven. The rice she'd cooked was keeping warm in the oven, and the sauce was on the stove. One week they'd been in Paradise Rocks, but it felt like a lifetime. He'd been working at the mechanic shop for a couple of days returning home stinking of engine fluid and covered in grease. Leaving the kitchen she cleaned away the mess from her day at home. Killer's one demand for her was to soak up the sun while he was at work.

She missed working as a dental nurse and wished there was a way for them to get back to their lives. Standing at the window she stared out over the lawn. The grass didn't need mowing. Her life was so boring.

When Killer got home, he'd go for a shower, then eat his dinner before they sat down watching movies. By the time they got to bed he'd hold her close and fall asleep. Nothing else happened between them.

"This fucking sucks," she said, cursing out like mad. She wanted Killer to touch her, to make love to her. The other day he'd taken her to the library, and she'd absorbed every sex scene she could find. Watching movies she hoped the love scenes they saw would spark something inside him. Instead he looked bored more than anything else.

Her wrists were healing. The plasters would be coming off in no time. Sandy was stopping by to check them over on Friday. She couldn't wait to have them come off.

Thumping the pillow she glared at her reflection. Her body was on fire, and she didn't even get to talk to Tate, who always calmed her down.

"Fuck, what did the pillow do?" Killer asked, catching her attention. Turning around she saw he'd come through the back door.

"Why did you come through the back door?" She stood up, pushing strands of hair off her face.

"I'm a mess." He opened his arms up for her to see all the mess. "I'm heading for a shower. We'll talk in a minute."

No, we won't talk. You'll eat, and then we'll watch a movie, and nothing will ever happen.

Ranting through her thoughts, she stamped her foot. Feeling childish, she headed back into the kitchen to finally serve them up some food. She tried to squash the feelings down. Killer tried more moves on her when they weren't alone. His touch always set her aflame.

I'm a twenty-six year old virgin.

Fuck, I almost died a virgin.

Tears filled her eyes at the uselessness of her situation. How could she beg him for sex? It wasn't in her style at all, yet it was all she could imagine. Her dreams were filled with his possessive touch. By the time morning came she was so turned on and shaken she left the bed before he could see her breaking apart for his touch.

She took out the chicken, served up two plates of food. Pouring the sauce over the meal she heard Killer enter the room.

"Something smells so good," he said, taking a seat.

Putting the plate in front of him, she waited for him to sit before grabbing her own plate and sitting next to him. Remaining silent, she ate without even looking at him. His cell phone buzzed, and he pulled it out to read the text.

The last thing she knew about Fort Wills and Michael was the fact they couldn't find the proof linking him to some underhanded dealings. Part of her hope they never found anything as that way she and Killer would be alone a lot longer.

"Alex is onto something. He's returning to Vegas to get something more. We could be back home before we know it."

Slamming her fork back on the table, she glared at Killer.

"Anything wrong?" he asked.

Growling in frustration, she stood up, chucked her food away and stomped away from him. She entered the sitting room staring at the pillow she'd been attacking earlier. Even though she felt like a child, she started hitting out, wishing it was something harder for her to break apart.

"What the hell is going on with you?" Killer asked, grabbing her around the arms, trapping them by her side.

Fighting him, Kelsey tried to break free of his hold. Stamping on his foot didn't achieve anything at all, and trying to sink her nails into his arms didn't help either.

"Stop!" He shouted the word. Wriggling in his arms, she finally stopped fighting and slumped. Only his hold on her kept her on her feet.

The moment he released her, she spun and

slapped him around the face. Raising her palm she went to hit him again, but he caught her wrist.

"Enough!"

"No, why did you bring me here? Why?"

He frowned. "What the fuck are you talking about?" he asked.

Her handprint stood out on his cheek. She got little satisfaction at the mark she'd given him. "You could have sent any of your men or even a fucking prospect to supervise me, so why did you have to come?"

"You're not making any sense at all." He placed a hand to her hand. Batting his touch away she glared at him. "Have you had too much sun today?"

"No, I've not had any sun. I'm just thinking clearly for the first time in weeks. God, I actually thought you *wanted* me. I was so fucking wrong it's not even funny anymore. The clothes, the movies, nothing is doing it for you, is it?" Her cheeks were on fire at her wicked thoughts.

Killer paused, staring at her and then past her shoulder. "I actually don't have a clue what you're talking about."

"God, I'm talking about sex. Why are you here when you clearly don't want to be with me?" She was shouting the words. Her hands flew all over the place in exasperation.

Silence fell between them at her admission.

Killer's answer was to laugh.

Seriously, he was laughing at her.

Hitting his chest, she slapped him hard hoping to shut him up.

Once again he caught her to him, stopping her from lashing out and hurting him everywhere. The way the bastard was treating her, he deserved a little pain. None of her emotions made any sense to her. She wanted

Killer, and yet he kept her at arms' length. Was she wrong to want him?

The laughter died as the first tear fell from her eyes.

Glaring at him she waited for more of his laughter. "Do you really think I don't want you?" he asked.

"You've not even tried to be with me. Why should I believe anything else?" she asked, tensing.

He cupped her cheek, tilting her head back to look into her eyes. "You really don't have a clue, do you?"

She remained silent hoping he'd put her mind at ease.

Killer shook his head.

"All of your education and a degree to your name, and you don't have a clue."

"If you're going to keep throwing my lack of knowledge in my face, let me go."

"No, I'm not letting you go at all." He slammed his lips down on hers moving his hands down to cup her ass. She gasped as he thrust his pelvis against her stomach. His cock was rock hard, pressing against the front of his jeans. Fingers sank into her hair, fisting the strands. Suddenly, he tugged on the length pulling her away from him. "You're going to realize something once and for all."

He walked her back until she was pressed against the far wall.

"You've been driving me fucking crazy. You don't think I want to fuck you." He didn't give her a chance to answer before he was talking again. "Every time I see you I'm hard as rock. All I want is to get your naked and fuck you. The moment I take your virginity I've got to give you time. I'm fucking big, Kels. I'm going to hurt you, but the moment I'm inside your tight little cunt I'm never going to want to stop." He covered her mouth with his hand. "No, you'll shut the fuck up and let me speak. I was being considerate to you. You tried to kill yourself, and I don't care if it's a mistake or not, I'm not going to try and fuck you so soon. I'm proving to you I want more, Kels. I'm treating you like a lady."

Licking her lips, she tasted his skin on her tongue. His cursing turned her on. The smoky look in his eyes made her feel alive.

"Do you want me to fuck you?" he asked.

He didn't withdraw his hand. She had no choice but to nod her head.

"You better make sure you know what you're agreeing to. The moment I get inside your fucking cunt I'm having it all. Once I pop your cherry, Kels, Michael will have no choice but to divorce you. I'll own every inch of you, and nothing is off the market. Do you get me?"

All he was doing was turning her on.

"This is your last chance to stop me."

She didn't say anything. Instead she stared into his eyes waiting for him to lose control.

"You've lost any chance of getting away." He pulled away, taking a seat on the sofa. Killer kicked the coffee table out of the way. "Get your clothes off. I want to see you naked."

There was no turning back now.

Chapter Twelve

Resting a hand on his leg Killer stared back at Kelsey waiting for her to make the next move. He'd been keeping his need at bay, masturbating in the shower twice a day to make sure he didn't pressure her. The anger she'd just unleashed gave him some kind of hope that she'd moved on from whatever negative thoughts had been claiming her.

"You want me to get naked."

"Yeah, the moment you do, I will fuck you."

He wasn't lying. Her clothes came off, and then he was fucking her pussy. It was only a matter of time before Alex got what they needed. When he got the proof they were heading back to Fort Wills to get Michael out of their lives. Once the divorce was done and completed he'd be making their marriage real.

She fingered the base of her shirt. Her hands were shaking, but he forced himself to stay still on the sofa. His cock pressed against his zipper begging to be released. No way was he getting his cock out until they were upstairs.

If his cock came out then there was no hope of being nice. He'd fuck her on the coffee table if he had to in order to get inside her.

The shirt came off revealing her tits bound in a white lace bra. He saw her large red nipples poking through. His mouth watered, and his cock pulsed even more. Resting his head on his hand, he waited for her to get rid of the rest of her clothing.

She pushed the jeans out, tucking her hair behind her ear as she went. Okay, she really was a full figured woman. The times he'd seen her naked he'd never gotten the chance to take his time watching her.

Rubbing his cock, he tried to ease the pain of the

zipper. She stood, hands clasped together in front of her.

"The rest."

"What?"

"Take your bra and panties off. I want to see you naked, Kels."

Hands still shaking, she reached behind her to remove the bra from her body. Cock hurting like hell, he waited for her to stand before him naked.

He recalled the men talking about their women going to the beauty salon. Looking at her pussy, he knew she kept her hair trimmed. There was a time she would get a wax along with Tate. Killer didn't much care for his woman having a bare pussy.

"Come here," he said.

She stepped between his legs. Reaching out, he placed a hand on her hip feeling her silky skin underneath his fingers. "Do you have any idea how fucking sexy you are?" he asked.

Kelsey shook her head. Moving her away from his legs he got her to open her thighs wide for him. Sliding a hand between her he cupped her pussy. She was soaking wet. Glancing up into her eyes he saw she was nervous.

She's a virgin. Remember that she's never done this before. Take your time. Go slow.

"Go upstairs to the bedroom," he said.

Watching her move away from him, he gave himself a few seconds to get his cock under control. He already had plenty of condoms and lubrication in the drawer beside his bed. The first morning he went out without her, he'd gone into the sex shop and bought them. There was nothing like having a good supply of condoms even though he wanted to feel her pussy bare around him. Would it be entirely wrong to fuck her without a condom?

She'd not been with anyone, and he was clean. The last check he had came up clean even though he'd been with the redhead since then.

Fuck. He cursed knowing he'd have to wear a condom until he got another check. He was sure he'd used a condom, but he couldn't be completely sure. Killer knew he'd rather wait than risk causing Kelsey more harm.

Locking the doors and windows, he got the house safe before heading upstairs to his woman. Once he got inside her, he knew they were not coming downstairs for some time. He worked tomorrow, but then it was the weekend, and for the weekend he'd fuck her.

As he headed upstairs, his cock tightened with every step he took.

Killer found her sitting on the edge of the bed, her hands locked together. She looked up at him with flushed cheeks. The curtain was drawn closed. No one would be able to see them, and he walked over to open the curtain letting in the natural light.

"You're not hiding from me, Kels. This is you and me."

Going to his belt, he began to open his jeans, shuffling them down his thighs to land on the floor. Removing his shirt, he walked to her side, naked and rock hard.

She gasped, her fingers sliding around his length.

"You're, erm, you're…" She didn't finish her words.

Tugging her to her feet, he looked down into her beautiful blue eyes. "I'm going to fit. Your pussy is made for me, and by the time I slide inside you, you're going to come apart." Leaning down, he tilted her head back, and he took possession of her lips. She moaned, her hands going to his stomach. Her fingers dug into his muscles. When she moved down to grip his cock, he stopped her.

"Why won't you let me touch you?" she asked.

"In time. I've fucked before. This is your first time." He nudged her back until she sat on the bed. Killer followed her down, forcing her to move back on the bed until she lay against the pillows.

Sliding his tongue along her lips, he waited for her to open. She did so, and he plundered her mouth, meeting her tongue with his own. Deepening the kiss, he caught her hip with his arm as he rested his other palm beside her head holding him up.

Kelsey melted against him, opening her thighs wide. When he was ready he'd fuck her, but until he got her prepared to receive him they were not doing either.

"Killer," she said, whimpering.

Kissing down her neck, he sucked on her pulse before moving around, across her collarbone. She writhed underneath him. Holding onto her hip, he kept her as steady as he needed her to be.

She chanted his name over and over again. Caressing down her body, he sucked in her left nipple before going to her right. She arched up, but he only touched her with his lips.

"Please," she said, begging. Ignoring her begging, he sucked on her nipples while stroking between her creamy folds. He slid a finger over her clit feeling her shudder.

Pulling back and resting on his legs, he opened her slit and stared down at her swollen clit. The sunlight was bright as it shone in the room giving him the perfect view of her creamy flesh. He was in heaven. Kelsey was more than he ever imagined.

"Killer?"

"You're beautiful. Have you ever seen your

creamy cunt?" he asked.

She shook her head. Withdrawing from the bed, he grabbed a mirror from the bathroom, returning to his position on the bed. "What are you doing? I can't look."

Kelsey settled back on the bed staring up at the ceiling.

"I'm not going to touch your pussy until you look at yourself."

"It's wrong."

"That's old-fashioned. My woman will know how beautiful her pussy is. Look."

He stayed still, holding the mirror in front of her pussy, waiting for her to do as he asked. Every woman had the right to see themselves.

She turned to look at him then down to the mirror.

"Look how perfect you are," he said.

"You're a strange man."

Laughing, he placed the mirror by the side of the bed. "You better get used to it. When we get our own place I'll be filling the place with mirrors so I can watch my cock sliding inside you."

Kelsey shook her head, pressing her hands to her cheeks.

"Get used to it, baby. I speak my mind."

"I know. I don't know how I'm ever going to survive."

"You've got no choice. You're mine now, and I'm not letting you go." He'd seen Lash, Murphy, Nash, and Tiny be possessive of their women. Now it was his turn to be that way with his. No man was ever going to take her away from him, not even Michael.

"Touch yourself," he said.

She hesitated, her hand resting on her stomach. Taking hold of her hand, he placed her palm to cover her pussy. Showing her how to touch herself, he watched her play with her clit. Kelsey cried out, getting braver and using two fingers to stroke her clit. He watched the light touch seeing from her response what she liked the most. When he could stand it no longer, he took hold of her hand and sucked the cream from her fingers. She was musky and sweet.

His cock jerked, knowing no other man had tasted her creamy flesh.

"What are you thinking?" she asked, frowning.

"No other man will ever know the taste of your sweet cunt."

Smiling, she opened her thighs, and he went down until his mouth was level with her slick heat. "What are you doing?"

"You're asking a lot of questions, baby. Close your eyes or watch me. I'm going to make you feel so good and scream my name when you come."

Opening the folds of her sex, he stared down at her virgin hole impatient to get inside her.

The scent of her arousal drove him insane. Leaning down he glided his tongue over her clit feeling her come apart. She sat up on the bed, but he kept touching her.

Slowly, she lay back down. Her hands held onto her thighs, almost as if she needed to keep herself grounded. Circling her clit, he changed the pace going from fast to slow. He took his time to suck the little button into his mouth. A little pain drove her wild, and he saw her creamy cum gliding down to coat her puckered hole. He'd be claiming her ass as well in time.

There was nothing they wouldn't do. Killer was going to show her *everything.*

"Killer, please," she said, begging him.

Knowing she wasn't going to be able to handle

much more, he caressed her clit not letting up until she screamed his name as her release took over. Removing his tongue, he used his fingers as he leaned over the bed to grab a condom from his drawer. Tearing into the foil packet, he slid the latex over his cock making sure to squeeze the tip before putting the condom on.

Moving over her, he rested his body weight on one hand while gripping his cock with the other. Sliding his covered cock through her slit, he coated the shaft with her cream. She was staring at him, taking deep breaths as she did.

"I love you, Kels." He pushed the tip of his cock to her entrance. Not waiting for her to grow accustomed to him, he slammed in deep in one thrust. She screamed, and he caught her fighting arms, locking them to the bed on either side of her head.

Though he hated the fact he caused her pain, the guilt was overridden by the pleasure of her tight cunt gripping him. He finally claimed Kelsey as his woman.

****

Killer was going to split her in two. Kelsey tried to fight him off, but he held her to the bed. The hard length of his cock was buried deep inside her, and she was burning with the width of his possession. He covered her body and she tried to push him off, but her weight was nothing compared to his.

"Get off," she said, sobbing at the pain.

"No, and be fucking still."

His cock pulsed harder inside her. Killer reared back, and she saw him glaring down at her. "Will you stop before you fucking hurt yourself?"

Pausing at the anger in his voice she finally stopped moving.

"Thank fuck."

"We can't do this. It hurts too much," she said,

trying to make him see reason.

"You don't think other women have felt this kind of pain?" he asked. His eyebrow was raised as he stared down at her. "Wait, Kels. This is your first time, and you're twenty-six. You've been a virgin for a long time."

"What does my age have to do with anything?" she asked, confused.

"Nothing. Just wait and stop trying to fight me. You're never going to win against me."

Wishing there was something else she could say to refute him, she stayed still feeling the pressure of his hands on top of hers.

She didn't want to think about how much she liked being held still. His touch was dominant and made her yearn for him to take control.

You're not thinking clearly.

Either way, she stared into his eyes. He didn't move at all even though she felt the hot brand of his dick inside her. Frowning, she started to feel something else. His cock stayed still, and she moved, thrusting up to him.

"I thought it was too painful for you?" he asked, mocking. An answering pulse started up inside her, begging to be known. Licking her lips she gazed up into his lust filled eyes. "Are you ready for me to move?"

"Please, be careful, I don't want it to hurt."

"I'm not going to hurt you, baby."

He leaned down sliding his tongue into her mouth. She opened up for him, moaning as he pulled his cock out of her. There was a slight burn from the movement but no longer any pain.

"There, now it feels good, doesn't it, baby?"

She nodded, gasping as he thrust inside her, going deep.

Wow, no wonder people love having sex.

"Do you want me to stop?" he asked, pausing

inside her.

"No, please don't stop."

"Tell me to fuck you, Kels," he said, nibbling on her neck.

"What?"

"You're not going to hide in the bedroom, baby. You're going to tell me what you want, or we're not going to get anywhere."

Biting her lip she did as he asked, begging him to fuck her. Killer didn't make her wait long before he gave her what she wanted. He glided inside her, speeding up his tempo until he pounded away. She could do nothing but hold on to him. The hard length of his cock burned her up with more pleasure than she could have ever imagined. Crying out, she felt his lips biting onto her nipples sending a riot of sensation through her whole system.

"That's it, baby. Come for me. Let me feel it around my fucking cock." He growled the words at her against her breast.

Killer gripped her hands, pressing them to the bed beside either side of her head. "Do you feel me?" he asked.

"Yes." She moaned as he slammed inside her, pausing. Kelsey felt every jerk and pulse of his cock deep within her core. Kelsey loved the way he held onto her. He held her trapped against the heat of his body, and she no longer wanted to fight him. The feel of his cock working inside her was pure bliss.

"You're mine, Kelsey. Tell me who you belong to."

"I belong to you." He didn't move, holding her down with his hands and cock buried deep inside her. She wanted him moving once again.

"No man will ever know how this virgin pussy

feels, baby. I own you, body, heart, mind, and fucking soul." He stared down at her, waiting.

"Yes. I love you."

"Good. You will divorce Michael Granito, and then you'll become my wife. Every night I will spend my time fucking, loving, and cherishing you."

"Yes." She smiled thinking about everything they were going to explore together. Minutes ago her body had protested to his touch whereas now she needed him to move. She craved his body. "Please, Killer," she said.

"Tell me what you want, Kels. There will be no hiding between us. When you want to come, you come to me and ask me to finger your pussy. You want my tongue on your body, you ask. If you need my cock, you come to me at all times and ask. I don't care what time of day it is, morning, noon, or fucking night, you come to me."

"You're not my sex slave."

"You are mine." He slammed his lips down on hers, drowning out any of her protests. Locking their fingers together, he drew out of her body. "Watch me," he said.

She glanced down seeing his latex covered cock appear between her thighs.

"I'm going to fuck you without a rubber very soon, baby. My cum is going to be inside you."

"What are you saying?" she asked, licking her lips to make it easier to speak.

"I want you to have my children, Kels. No more women, no more men, and no more fucking secrets. You don't want me to meet your parents, that's fine, but you will tell me about them. There is going to be true fucking honesty. This is what I want." He kissed down her neck, and she tensed at the overload of sensation swimming inside her body.

Every inch of her body felt drawn to the pinnacle of pleasure but could not be thrown over the edge. Killer kept her balanced controlling everything he did, bringing her more and more pleasure.

"Scream for me, baby."

He pulled out and slammed inside her, each thrust creating a mixture of pleasure and pain with the depths of his invasion. In no time at all she screamed her pleasure, whimpering at her need to orgasm.

"Come for me." Leaving one of her hands free beside her head, he caressed her clit, bringing her to new heights of lust. The feel of his fingers caressing her nub while he fucked her at the same time were entirely different and amazing.

There was no control, and within seconds he had her hurtling over the edge. She gripped his shoulder trying to hold onto him in order to ground her. Through her orgasm she felt him find his own release, grunting as it came.

Their cries mingled on the air, and she felt so connected to him for the first time in ages.

"I love you. I love you. I love you." She needed him to know how much he meant to her. Every waking moment drew her closer to him.

"Baby, words are not enough anymore." He kissed her lips, collapsing over her. Wrapping her arms around his waist, she held onto him. His weight hurt, but she wanted to keep him in her arms for as long as possible.

"No, I've got to get up. I don't want to hurt you."

"It's no pain at all," she said.

Still, he withdrew, pulling out of her body and away from her arms. He reared back to glare down. His fingers slid across her pussy, moving the fine hairs.

"What is it? What's the matter?" she asked, going

to her elbows to see what he was looking at.

"You've got a little bit of blood. I'm, erm, I'm going to grab a towel to clean it away." He pulled away from the bed leaving her alone.

She was a virgin. There should be a small amount of blood. He returned carrying a damp cloth. The frown on his face unnerved her.

"Are you all right?" she asked, biting her lip.

"Yeah, I'm fine."

In a matter of minutes he'd withdrawn from her again. "Killer, look at me," she said, trying to gain his attention.

The cool cloth was pressed between her thighs wiping away the blood.

"I never want to hurt you," he said, through gritted teeth. Her heart went out to him.

Jerking out from under him, she went to her knees by his side. Cupping his cheek, she stared into his dark gaze. "Look at me," she said.

He did as she asked, staring into her eyes.

"You didn't hurt me."

"You fucking fought me, Kels. Don't try and lie to me."

"I was a virgin, okay. It hurt for you to be inside me that first time. Every woman feels some kind of discomfort the very first time. I felt it a lot. Please, don't make this about you. You weren't a virgin, and you're not a woman." Kissing his lips, Kelsey realized she'd never been happier in her life. "Do you see how wonderful you've made this?"

"I like it rough, Kels."

"So?"

"I like it rougher than we just had."

She smiled. "This was my first time. I think I'll be on the same wavelength as you in no time." Kelsey knew, even though she was a little frightened, she'd do whatever it took to keep Killer in her life.

On the outside, he was a tough man, a criminal to most. She knew on the inside, he loved more greatly than any saint. His love for the club, his brothers, and her was absolute. Nothing could make him change.

She wouldn't want to change him and looked forward to exploring a hell of a lot more with him.

****

"They're looking for her, Sir," Daniel said.

Michael glanced up from the paperwork for the business he really wanted. "What?" he asked, wishing he heard wrong.

"Your enemies know about your wife. They also know she was in the hospital near Fort Wills. They're looking for her."

Daniel was his most trusted friend and the head of his security.

Anger gripped him, and he lifted the coffee table throwing it away from him. "Fuck, after all this time, one fucking slip up and they're onto her."

"Got news through the grapevine, they've got a picture of her as well."

His enemies were not his. They were another fucking inheritance he didn't want from his father. If he could have given this piece of shit business of finding, kidnapping, and selling girls he'd have handed it over to them years ago. The problem he faced was that handing over such a business came at a price. The only way out of trafficking girls was to end up six feet in the ground. Michael liked his life and wasn't prepared to die even when he hated elements of his life. Selling girls had never appealed to him.

Marrying Kelsey had been a mistake, but he had no choice to inherit his father's wealth. It was only a few months after marrying her that he realized the true extent of his father's evil. Michael would not have her death on his conscience like so many other girls. If Kelsey ended up dead it was only going to be a matter of time before he had with The Skulls after him. What the fuck was he supposed to do when faced with those kinds of odds?

"We need to find them before they do," Michael said, pacing.

"This is out of your area, Sir. You're going to have to trust The Skulls with this one. They already know where she is."

He shook his head. "No, I can't trust them."

Daniel sighed. "I know it's not what you wish to do, but you're not in any position to keep yourself back. This is a matter of survival, hers as well as yours."

Running fingers through his hair, Michael felt ready to explode with anger. He wasn't in the mood for trusting people. Look at what happened from trusting his father. All the years he'd taken over their legitimate business for his father to retire early, and instead he'd got drawn into human trafficking, slave trading. The thought alone made him feel sick to his stomach. Then he found out two of the staff were purchased from his father and ordered to do as he wished. Michael set them free. He never took any unwilling woman, which was why he had left Kelsey alone.

"Get on to your sources. Killer would not have gone far. Find anything you can," Michael said, trying to plan around the problems knocking at his door.

"Will do, sir. I want to warn you it's only a matter of time before they find her."

He refused to believe his enemies would get to her before he did. Shit, the only consolation to his guilt was knowing that Killer would do everything in his power to keep her safe.

Chapter Thirteen

On Friday morning Killer rolled over, stretching out the sleep from his joints, not that he'd gotten much sleep. Smiling, he saw Kelsey was passed out beside him. Ever since taking her virginity he'd not given her a single moment of rest when they were together. While he worked at the shop with Mason was all the time away from her he needed. Most nights he left dinner to bend Kelsey over the table and pound into her from behind. He was making up for a lot of lost time.

His cock stirred remembering the feel of her lips wrapped around his shaft last night. Kelsey was insatiable. Her lust matched his in every way. They were perfect for each other.

Reaching out, he stroked a hand down her back loving the feel of her skin against his fingertips.

"Leave me alone," she said, muttering against the pillow. Pushing the hair off her back, he kissed down her spine, licking a path the further down he went. She moaned but made no move to fight him. Lifting her onto her knees, he opened the lips of her pussy to see her cunt glinting at him.

The puckered hole of her anus stared at him. He wanted to claim her ass as much as he'd claimed everything else.

His cock was rock hard already, and he couldn't wait to fuck her.

"Get a condom," he said, sliding his tongue into her juicy cunt.

Her cream exploded on his tongue the instant he slid inside her. Gathering her juice onto his fingers, he slid them back to press against her ass.

She tensed up but threw the foil packet in easy reach of him.

"Shall I stop?" he asked. Her ass was tight, and he had to put some pressure to get the tip of his finger inside her ass.

"No!"

Chuckling, he slid down to lap at her clit. He felt like a starving man needing to get another hit from her essence.

"Killer," she said, moaning.

Sliding his finger deep into her ass he withdrew to press back inside, getting her used to the feel of him inside her.

"Does that feel good?" he asked.

"Yes."

"You like my finger in your ass?"

"Yes."

Adding a second finger he tongued her pussy going from her pussy to her clit, teasing her with his ministrations. She grunted then whimpered as he brought her to the peak but withdrew completely. Her juices coated his chin, and he wiped them away.

With the two fingers inside her ass, he sawed them, trying to stretch her out to take him.

When he could stand it no longer, he removed his fingers and left to go to the bathroom. He quickly washed his hand shouting for her to stay in position for him. Grabbing the tube of lubrication from under the sink, he entered the bathroom to find her still on her knees.

"Good girl," he said, sliding his fingers across the cheeks of her ass.

"You're making it hard for me to think."

"Don't think. It's a waste of time here."

Tearing open the foil packet, he slid the latex over his cock before placing the tip of his cock inside her. He watched her pussy open up taking all of his cock. Sliding all the way inside he groaned feeling each ripple of her pussy. She was fucking heaven, the perfect combination of pleasure and pain for him.

Gripping her hips, he tightened his grip knowing his touch would leave bruises. He couldn't wait. Seeing the marks of his possession on her skin drove him insane. All he wanted to do was mark her so every man who saw her knew who she belonged to.

Staying still within her depths, he grabbed the lube and put plenty onto his fingers. The only way he was going to get inside her tight, hot ass was to get her ready to take him.

"Killer," she said, moaning.

She tried to thrust back against him. He slapped her ass, stopping her. "Don't move until I tell you to."

Kelsey cried out, muttering. He landed another spank to her ass. "I'm going to make you feel good in no time. Stop trying to force my hand." He warned her, refusing to move.

"Fine, you win."

"The more you realize I win all the time, the better it will be."

She blew a raspberry, which he found adorable. He knew exactly what would shut her up.

Taking his lubed fingers, he slid them over her puckered ass not pressing for more.

"You're driving me crazy," she said.

Using one lubed finger he slid into her ass without stopping. She cried out, wriggling on his cock.

Chuckling, he kept a firm hold of her hip with the other hand, digging the tips of his fingers into her skin. Bruises, he wanted to mark her for all to see.

Determined to get what he wanted, he dug in deeper as she took the second finger in her ass.

"I'm going to get you ready to take my cock, baby," he said, sliding his fingers in and out. Her pussy was so fucking wet.

She held him like a fist, tightening around his fingers and cock.

When he could take no more he pulled out of her cunt only to slam back inside. It was awkward, fucking her ass with his fingers and her pussy with his cock, but Killer loved a challenge.

"Please," she said, begging him.

"Touch yourself. I want to feel you come before I do."

He slammed into her over and over. She touched her clit, and Kelsey splintered apart. Killer loved how she never tried to lie to him, pretending to come when she actually hadn't. Some women got off on that. Killer thought it was ridiculous. Why fake an orgasm when he was more than prepared to give them the real deal?

Shoving all thoughts of other women out of his mind, he concentrated on her sweet cunt swallowing him up.

Soon, he'd take her without a condom. Sandy was stopping by the mechanic shop to take some blood to run tests for him, which he was thankful for. The last few days had become a nightmare. Many times he pulled away before he actually fucked her naked.

"So fucking tight. My pussy." He screwed her hard, not caring about anything but his own orgasm.

He felt her reach her second as he growled out his first. Kelsey was far better than his fist. Removing his fingers from her ass, he removed his cock, picked her up and carried her into the shower.

"You've got to stop picking me up like this," she complained. Turning the water on, he chuckled as she squealed at the cold.

Riding himself of the condom, he threw it in the trash before joining her.

"You've not even kissed me this morning." She pouted up at him.

Her wrists were getting wet, but he wasn't concerned. The wounds were healed, and Sandy was coming to check them out later that day.

Sinking his fingers into her hair he tilted her head back. "Then I better make up for it now." He pressed her against the cold tile, slamming his lips down on hers before she said another word.

Her moans were answer enough. She touched his stomach, her fingers dancing down to grip his hardening cock. "Please," she said.

When she'd sucked on him before, he always made sure to wear a condom before she took him into her mouth. "No, not until I'm sure of everything first." He kissed her lips. It was the only thing he allowed until he got a clean bill of health.

Kissing her hard, he washed her body before helping her out.

He left her to dress, to grab the jeans he left downstairs in the sitting room the night before. Killer had taken to leaving condoms in every room. They fucked whenever the need hit them.

Dressing in jeans and a shirt, he put the coffee pot on before getting himself some cereal. He had to work in twenty minutes, and he didn't want to be late.

Kelsey wore a yellow summer dress with a cardigan to cover the white plasters over her wrists.

"What time will you be home tonight?" she asked.

"I should be back by five thirty. We've got the weekend to ourselves, so be ready to be fucked every chance I get."

She chuckled, pouring a coffee for herself.

"Are you coming to town?" he asked.

"No, I'm going to soak up the sun until Sandy comes. Who is dropping her off?"

"Stink or Zero I think. Neither man wants to stick around the club at the moment." He placed his empty bowl in the sink, finishing off his coffee.

"Will they be staying the night?"

"No, they're staying for dinner but will be on the road in no time. We need to be hidden until Alex comes back with information."

"What is Michael doing? Do you know if he's sending police out looking for us or if he's just leaving us alone?" she asked, glancing down into her cup.

He wondered how to answer. The truth was the best course of action. "He confronted Tiny at the club the day after. No police have gotten involved, but he's still in Fort Wills. Some of our men are onto him. Do you miss him?"

"No. I'm more worried for us."

"Don't be, baby. I've got to get going. See you soon." He kissed her head, forcing himself to leave the house before he stayed. Leaving Kelsey after everything that happened was getting harder and harder each day.

****

"Are you sure he's fine sitting outside?" Kelsey asked, looking out the open door to see Stink on his cell phone.

"Yeah, he doesn't like watching me play doctor." Sandy removed the white plasters that covered her scars. "This is perfect. The scars will be minimal but can't be helped." She assessed the marks in detail. "Providing you're not doing dirty work, I think it's best to leave them open. It will help for them to heal faster."

Kelsey waited for Sandy to finishing cleaning them before talking again. Resting her hands in her lap, she stared at the other woman as she packed her case away.

"How are Tate and the others?"

"Tate's fine. She's her usual bossy self. I love her, but she's driving the men crazy with her fears. She wanted to come today and so did Zero, but Stink wouldn't let them." Sandy shrugged. "Everyone is on lockdown. I think Alex might have found something out. There was a call last night, but none of the men are saying anything. They're keeping it all to themselves being all secretive."

Sandy called Stink in to take the case back out to the car. The other man wasn't wearing his leather cut either. Kelsey asked why.

"This is a new threat, and until they all know what's going on, the men don't leave Fort Wills with a cut. Stink hates it, but he wouldn't let Zero take his place." Sandy rested her head on her palm.

"Why does Zero want to come here?" Kelsey asked, pleased to be talking to people she knew. Tate was her best friend, but she'd take whatever friendship she could get.

"He's on lockdown with Sophia. Man is in love with her." Sandy rolled her eyes. "He tries to hide it."

Kelsey knew about Zero's infatuation with Sophia. Tate talked about it often.

"What about you, Kels? How is married life treating you?"

Laughing, Kelsey stared down at the ring on her ring finger. "It's pretty perfect."

"I recognize that glow, honey. Killer fucking you good, is he?"

Heat filled her cheeks. Sandy's words embarrassed her, especially when Stink chuckled on his way back.

"Can't you keep anything to yourself?" Kelsey

asked.

"Come on, I want details. I've stopped being a fuck buddy to the men. It's my own choice, but I need details, lots and lots of details," Sandy said.

Rolling her eyes, Kelsey stood to make a cup of tea. "Killer says you're staying for dinner?"

"Yeah, I've already stopped by to take his blood."

"What? Why would you need to take Killer's blood?" Kelsey started to worry about the man she'd been staying with. How had she not known something was wrong with him? She felt like such an awful girlfriend. *Girlfriend?* Was she a girlfriend?

Crap, her thoughts were getting too far ahead of her.

"Girl, he wants to be clean so he can fuck you without a condom."

Okay, her cheeks were going to set on fire if Sandy kept talking bluntly. "What?"

"Don't be worried. I'll do the tests, but Killer wants to get rid of the rubber. He's staking his claim over you, and it's only a matter of time before you're his old lady with a ring on your finger that means the same." Sandy stood, stretching out her muscles. "God, I've been sitting for a long time in that blasted car."

"You can go for a walk if you want around the garden. I'm going to get dinner ready for when Killer's off work." Kelsey stood, making two coffees for her guests. Stink took both cups from her as Sandy was stretching out in the garden.

She saw the lust in the other man's gaze, directed entirely at Sandy.

"Cheers, doll."

"You're welcome." Kelsey hated calling him Stink and made herself scarce. The look in his eyes made her feel frozen to the spot. Did Sandy know that the man wanted her?

It wasn't her place to tell Sandy what she knew.

Concentrate on my own business.

She pulled the steaks out of the fridge to get to room temperature as she made a mixture to stuff into the beef. Every now and then she stared outside wondering about the strange couple. Sandy was so independent while Stink seemed closed off. Neither of them looked ready to open up to the other.

Getting back to her work, she rolled the stuffing into the steaks, placing them in a pot covering them with tomatoes and herbs before putting the pot into the oven. All she needed to do was cook some pasta, toss together some salad, and dinner was made.

Glancing at the clock she saw Killer was going to be home within the hour. She stepped outside to soak up what little bit of sun she could.

Stink was on the phone a lot of the time while Sandy took in the sun. "Man, this is the life. With lockdown we're not allowed outside unless accompanied by one of the crew. It gets dull having a man watch over you."

"Killer's orders were getting some sun."

"You're not tanned enough, Kels. You've got to learn to show a bit of skin off to get what you want."

Sandy had her eyes closed, stretched out on one of the loungers. Her skirt was up around her waist as her shirt lay open exposing her modest bra.

"I can't just get naked," she said.

"You'd be surprised what you can do, honey. Me, I didn't think it was possible to be confident as I got older, but look at me. I fuck who I want, and I'm not exactly in my early twenties. I'm in my late thirties, and I'm not telling you my exact age either."

Kelsey chuckled. "Don't be concerned about your

age. Stink certainly doesn't mind your age."

Sandy opened her eyes, shielding them from the sun with a palm to her forehead. "What are you going on about?" she asked.

"Stink. He's got feelings for you."

It was Sandy's time to laugh. "No, honey, you've got that completely wrong. He doesn't want anything to do with me. Tiny gave him the job of looking after me. It's all he's doing."

Kelsey wanted to dispute the other woman, but Killer walked out the back door covered in his overalls, which were thick with grease.

"Hey, man, ladies. I'm going to wash up, and I'll be out to join you." Killer left without another word.

"Wow, isn't this domestic bliss if ever I saw it," Sandy said.

"Stop it. I better finish up dinner."

Leaving the two in the garden, Kelsey filled a pot with water and started to prepare the salad along with several other items. She set the table for the four of them, then drained the pasta. When she got to the salad, Killer stepped up behind her.

"I'm clean now, baby." He kissed her neck, sucking on her pulse. "Fuck, I missed you." His hands banded around her waist, drawing her back against his cock. She felt the hard length on his cock against her ass. He moaned then reached up to cup her breast. "Wish they were gone. I'd fuck you right now before we eat."

She wanted that. Closing her eyes, she crossed her legs feeling heat spill into her panties.

Stink cleared his throat making them aware of his presence. She jumped at the sudden intrusion while Killer laughed but didn't pull away immediately.

"Sorry," Stink said. "I didn't mean to interrupt."

"Yes, you did." Killer pulled away, dropping a

kiss to her neck as he left.

Out of the corner of her eye she saw him go to the fridge withdrawing some juice.

Once they were all around the table, Kelsey visibly relaxed.

"Dude, you're serving us juice?" Stink asked.

"If you were sticking around you'd get beer, but seeing as you're leaving I'm not going to spend my night worrying about you. I've got many other things planned for this evening," Killer said, reaching out to cup the back of her neck.

She smiled at him, feeling a tightening deep in her core. Killer knew what to say to make her melt for him.

The dinner went really well. Sandy and Stink complimented her food in between Killer asking questions about the club and life outside of the house.

Whenever Michael's name was brought up she couldn't help but get nervous. She'd married a man whom she knew nothing about. Most women would laugh at her stupidity.

A couple of hours later they stood together waving at their departing friends. Kelsey wished they were going along with them. She hated being away from Tate and Fort Wills. There were times she missed being a dental nurse.

Killer tugged her back into the house, kissing her neck. "We'll be leaving soon, I guarantee it."

"How? How can you guarantee it?" she asked.

He slammed the door closed and pressed her against the wall. She gasped as he tore the straps of her dress down her shoulders. "Sandy told me you got the all clear." He lifted her hands to rest the palms against the wall.

"Yes."

"Good. I can't stand you being in pain."

Down the dress went landing at her feet. Next he rid her of the bra and then her panties. "Now, it's time for us to make up for lost time."

****

"They're in a small town called Paradise Rocks," Daniel said, entering the hotel room. Michael stood feeling terror grip him. If they knew where Kelsey and Killer were living then his enemies would also know the truth.

"How do you know?"

"Our men followed Sandy and Stink. They were not very clever in shaking them off." Daniel held up his cell phone showing a picture of the happy couple.

The picture was like a kick to the gut. Kelsey looked so bloody happy, and it wasn't because of him. He'd really thought he could get her to stay married to him. She never argued, until recently, and he liked the idea of having a wife who would let him do what he wanted. Michael liked variety in his women.

"Arrange a meeting with *them*. I want to keep them off her scent as long as possible." Wiping a hand down his face, Michael started to panic.

Shit, fuck, shit.

Not only had Kelsey been discovered and her name linked with his but also Alex had found out the fucking truth. Michael believed he'd buried any paperwork linking his name to the trafficking. It was only a matter of time before The Skulls knew the truth. Maybe death would have been a better way to end his life.

"Sir, they're not answering," Daniel said.

Both men froze as the hotel's door was slammed open and a bleeding member of their security team was gasping for breath. Michael recognized the young man as

Ben, the one who helped to dispose of the girl shot in the head, the same man he posted outside of Kelsey's door. "We've been betrayed. The girls are gone. Eric and Mark are dead. They got a call, and the next moment they started shooting."

Ben collapsed to the floor, bleeding out.

Cursing, Michael got to the business of getting Ben to the hospital. It wasn't the brightest move he made. Sitting in the hospital, Michael looked at all of his problems. If he didn't act Kelsey would be dead like a long line of girls before her, and if they took Killer's life, he'd have The Skulls on his back.

Running a hand down his face, Michael weighed up his options.

There was no other option. The only way to get out of this alive was to bring The Skulls in.

"Daniel, call Tiny, the leader of The Skulls MC. It's time for us to get some help."

For Kelsey and Killer's sake, he hoped he wasn't too late.

Chapter Fourteen

Killer kissed down Kelsey's neck and bit into each cheek of her ass. Her cries made him rock hard. Spinning her around, he stared up her naked body taking in her full curves and heavy tits. He was one lucky bastard to have such a treasure to call his own.

Lifting her leg up, he stared at her pretty swollen cunt. She was already slick, ready for his cock.

Going up, he slid his tongue over her clit then down to slide into her pussy. He sucked her cum, swallowing her down.

She shuddered in his arms, struggling to stay up. The drawer unit nearest the door held some of his condoms. He took a condom out, opened his jeans taking out his erection. The tip was leaking out his pre-cum ready for action. Groaning, he put the condom on, wishing he didn't have to wear them.

Soon.

Spinning her back to face the wall, he tilted her hips out finding her heat. Sliding a finger into her core, he added a second then a third, pumping away inside her. Her pleasured cries turned to screams. Taking his cock in hand, he slid the tip against her, finding her entrance. Holding both of her hips in his hands, digging his fingers into her flesh, he slammed in deep.

He felt the tip hit her cervix, as he went as deep as he could.

"Fuck, I've been thinking about this all day," he said, pulling out only to slam back inside. Her palms were flat against the wall along with her cheek.

Killer gritted his teeth, but the pleasure was too much. He fucked her hard, never letting up in his need to fuck her.

Reaching around, he fingered her clit, strumming

the bud. Each touch had her cunt clutching him tighter.

She grew tighter as he stroked her clit.

"I want you to come around my cock, baby."

Pounding away inside her, he caressed her nub feeling her splinter apart. She screamed, the sounds echoing off the walls. He wanted to pound his chest with pride at her squeals.

Slamming inside her, Killer stared down at where his cock was sliding inside and out, the latex covered in her release. He couldn't wait to see his cock coated in her cum. Until then he'd make do with what he got.

Over and over, he fucked her against the wall. Kelsey plunged into her second release, and he finally found his, tightening his grip on her hips and groaning out.

Once it was over he felt utterly drained.

Kissing her neck, Killer kept his eyes closed loving the after feeling of the passion they'd shared.

Kelsey was the first woman he ever kept around after sex. Before he found her, most women were fucked and ordered out of his room. He kept Kelsey close by his side.

"We just did it near the front door. What if someone could see us?" Kelsey asked, sounding breathless.

"I'd argue with the postman for being late." He kissed her neck, sucking on her pulse, which pounded against his tongue.

"You're going to give me a hickey if you keep sucking on my neck."

"So? I want the whole world to see how much you turn me on. Every time you leave the house, you're going to be covered in my mark." He stroked the bruises decorating her hips.

Pulling out of her heat, he tapped her ass. "I'll

shut the curtains. I know you're nervous walking around naked when there's a risk others will see." Killer also didn't want any other man to see what belonged to him. Kelsey was his woman, and he didn't share.

Removing the condom he watched her slink off to the kitchen. Closing the curtains he stripped down, wiping his cock with the clothes. He found Kelsey doing the dishes, naked.

Sitting at the table, he watched her loving the jiggle of her ass as she moved.

"Are you not going to help me?" she asked.

She wore a pair of yellow gloves. Sandy had warned him she needed to keep the marks clear of any dirt.

"Sure, why not."

He walked toward her, drying up the dishes. Kelsey was a fantastic cook, and he knew he'd hit the jackpot in falling for her.

They worked in silence. Every now and then he gazed down admiring her large tits with full nipples.

When they were finished, he took her hand leading her into the sitting room. Closing up the curtains he set up the DVD with the latest romance movie. His life had been about crime, death, and horror. He didn't need to watch it to know it existed.

"We're watching a movie?" she asked.

Settling down on the sofa, he pulled her between his thighs, resting her against him.

"Yeah, we've got all the time in the world to fuck. I just want to hold you while we do something together." Killer stroked his hand up and down her arm.

"This is nice," she said, sighing.

They were both completely naked, and Killer smiled at his lies. Yes, he wanted them to watch something together, but he also wanted to spend the entire movie caressing her glorious body. She rarely did anything naked, but he'd got her relaxed enough to do this with him. The movie started up, and he rested a palm on her stomach while his other caressed her neck.

Her hair rested down one side covering one of her tits. Glaring at the offending hair, he moved it out of the way so the length covered him rather than his view of her tits.

The movie played, and he didn't care for the storyline or anything else. His attention was split between her tits and her pussy. He stroked his fingers across her stomach feeling her quiver.

Her nipples hardened, silently begging him to suck on them.

Closing his eyes, he tried not to be obvious in his need to fuck her rather than watch the movie.

"You're not watching the movie at all," Kelsey said, ten minutes later.

"I am."

"No, you're not. I feel how hard you are, Killer. Also, I feel your eyes on me rather than looking at the television."

"So, I like looking at you."

"This is a fluke. You did this so you could touch me without leading straight to sex."

"Oh, this is going to lead to sex, just not straight away." He stayed still on the sofa while she made to turn toward him. Pressing his hand on her stomach, he stopped her from moving.

"Stop moving." He ordered her, holding her down. "We'll fuck soon. Let me play."

She murmured something, which he didn't care to hear, but she stayed still.

For the next hour he played with Kelsey's body not even trying to hide his need for her. Kelsey remained silent.

He circled her nipples watching them bud up. Her breathing deepened with every second that passed. Not letting up, he moved to the next nipple while also teasing the fine hairs decorating her pussy.

She opened her legs for him to touch her easily. He didn't touch her pussy until he was damn good and ready.

Half way through the movie she growled in frustration, closing her thighs once again.

Chuckling, he stroked her neck, feeling her pulse pound against his fingertips.

"I'm not liking you at all at the moment."

"Baby, I'm not here to be liked, but if you can forgive me then I'll take it."

Kelsey turned around and stuck her tongue out.

Laughing, he finished watching the movie, caressing her body as he did. When the movie finally came to a close, he knew her body was tense with arousal. Turning the television off, he took her hand leading her upstairs to their room. The sun had gone down, and he switched the light on so he could watch her response to him.

Turning her around, he pulled her close feeling her plump tits press against his front. "Beautiful," he said, claiming her lips again.

"Please." She wrapped her arms around his neck, pouting. "I need you to fuck me."

"Not yet. We're going to take it slow tonight." He ran his hands up and down her back, loving her frustration.

She didn't move away from him, resting her head against his chest. He loved her bare wrists. Taking each palm he laid a light kiss to her scars.

"I love you," she said.

"I know." Tilting her head back, he took possession of her lips. She opened up to his invading tongue.

Tasting her lips, he plundered her mouth meeting her tongue with his.

They kissed, running their hands up and down each other's bodies for many minutes. Killer didn't care how much time he spent with her in his arms. No time spent together would ever be long enough to him.

Seeing Sandy and Stink had made him ache to be back with the club. Until Michael was dealt with the only hope he had was keeping her safe in this small town.

No one was going to find them. He took every care in keeping her safe.

Breaking the kiss, he sucked on her neck then knelt down to take each nipple into his mouth in turn.

"You're driving me crazy," she said, biting her lip. Kissing her stomach he moved her back to land on the bed.

He opened her thighs, watching her pretty pussy grow slick with arousal. Sucking her clit into his mouth, he tasted her cum and flicked her clit before sliding down to plunder her cunt.

She cried out, reaching down to grip his hair. With his hands on her hips, he slurped up her juice loving the noises he created inside her.

Kelsey begged him to let her come.

Circling her clit, he grazed over the nub bringing her to the edge but never letting her over. Keeping her release from her, he slid two fingers inside her pussy watching her swallow him up.

Her legs were shaking with each second that passed.

When he bit down on her nub he heard her scream. Knowing she couldn't take much more, he sucked her clit then flicked it until he heard and felt her release. Her cunt gripped his fingers tightly as her cum washed over the digits.

Killer brought her through the orgasm, bringing her down slowly. When he finished, he moved away, wiping her cream from his chin. He'd never get bored of licking her pussy.

Taking a condom and some lube from the drawer, he moved to the bed, helping her into the center.

Covering her lips with his own, he plundered her mouth once again feeling her respond to him.

"I love you," he said.

"I love you, too."

****

His fingers went around her neck, touching her pulse. Kelsey stared into his eyes seeing the flash of lust burning bright within his depths. She'd give him everything. Her love for him never wavered. Some time ago, she had doubted for many weeks that she was strong enough to stay by his side. Now, she knew she was.

Killer meant everything to her, and there was nothing she wouldn't do to keep him by her side. He had forgiven her over her mistake, but that was now in the past. Killer knew the truth, and she wouldn't be keeping anything else from him. She loved his brand of possession. The way he gripped her hips until she bruised, turned her on. When she was in his arms, she felt beautiful and cherished.

Down his hand went to circle her nipples.

Glancing at his cock, she saw he was rock hard. Through the whole of the movie he'd been turned on.

She wanted to give him the kind of pleasure he gave her all the time. Not once did he leave her wanting. During her time with him, she'd flourished under his care, and she couldn't wait to tell Tate everything.

Going to him, she pressed her hands on his chest and leaned down to kiss his lips. They were hard to the touch, but she loved the feel of him caressing her body. Licking his bottom lip like he did with her, she waited for him to open. Seconds later he opened his lips giving her access to his mouth.

Plunging her tongue into his mouth she moaned, feeling another wave of arousal grip her from his touch. His hands gripped the cheeks of her ass tightly, holding her against him.

"You're not taking charge here, Kels."

"I'm not wanting to take charge." She rubbed her nose against his. "We're playing, remember?" She smiled down at him.

His chuckle was a delight to hear. In one swift move he changed their positions and she was underneath him.

"Hey, I was going to make love to you for a change."

"No, you're going to take what I'm about to give you."

The condom and tube of lubrication weren't lost on her. Staring up at him, she circled his waist with his legs. His cock lay between her slit, making her yearn for him to fuck her.

"You're insatiable," he said.

"It's all your fault." She tried to fight his hand on her hands, but Killer was too strong. There was no chance of her escaping him. Only when Killer was ready to let her go would she be free.

"Stop fighting. You're not going anywhere."

His dark gaze held her steady. She waited for him to make the next move. Taking several deep breaths, she gazed at him, loving the feel of his hard body surrounding her.

Killer leaned down, taking her lips.

Her body was no longer her own. Killer owned every part of her. He licked, sucked, and nibbled on her body. When he pressed a kiss to her clit she almost came apart. He didn't give her the chance to grow accustomed to his touch before he used his massive body weight to turn her to her knees. Kneeling on the bed, she felt him reach over her to grab the condom and lube.

For some reason the first time they met hit her. Tate had introduced him to her. She remembered staring up at him being struck by the instant shock of arousal. Kelsey had never actually seen him before, but her body instantly recognized him. The attraction had shocked her at first as no other man made her feel that way. The time she spent with him had made her fall for him harder.

Knowing Michael was out there she'd tried to keep Killer far away from her. It hadn't worked at all. She missed him constantly. Seeing Tate reminded her of what she was missing, which only made her misery worse.

His hands caressed her ass, opening the cheeks and pulling her away from the memory. She couldn't believe how much their life had changed since that one meeting. Killer treated her with kindness most times.

Only when Michael had come to light did he treat her differently, and she'd deserved every harsh word he'd thrown her way. Keeping her marriage a secret was her biggest regret.

Killer stopped touching her. She heard the foil packet being torn into. Closing her eyes, she imagined him sliding the condom over his rock hard dick. He was long, thick, and the vein along the side would stick out harshly.

"What are you thinking about?" he asked.

"Nothing."

"You're lying. I see the evidence of your arousal. Try again."

Rolling her eyes, she moaned as his fingers slid through her pussy. "I'm thinking about you putting the condom on. You're very big. It always looks like you won't fit into a condom."

He chuckled. "Soon I'll take you without wearing a fucking condom. I hate them. I want to feel you wrapped around my dick with nothing between us."

She wanted it, too. There was so much she wanted to experience with him. "I'm not fucking your pussy, Kels. Tonight, I'm claiming your ass."

Killer spread the cheek of her ass open wide. Resting her head on her arms, she waited for him to finish what he was doing.

"I'm going to coat my fingers with the lube and then coat my cock before I start fucking you," he said.

"Talk me through everything you're doing." She loved hearing his voice and knew it would be a lot easier if he told her everything as it happened.

Her hearing was on high alert. She listened for the sound of the cap opening. Once it did, she tensed.

"Shh, don't worry about a thing. You're going to love what I do to you."

His hand went to the base of her back, stroking the muscles. She didn't relax thinking about that large cock trying to get into such a small hole.

Tate had talked about anal sex. When her friend started talking sex, she tuned out. She loved Tate, but some things she really didn't need to know. Right now she was wishing she'd listened to her friend. Instead, she was facing the unknown, and Killer was a big man.

"I'm covering my cock with the lube. I know you're going to be worried, but I promise you, Kels, I'll make this more than good." He stopped, and she turned to the side to see his fingers sliding a lot of clear gel over the latex. "You'll be begging for your ass to be fucked in no time."

She didn't have the heart to deny him.

Something cool and slightly hard pressed to her ass. "That's the tube. I'm using plenty. We've done this with my fingers, but I've never taken it further."

Suddenly, Kelsey didn't want him to speak. His voice soothed her, but his words made her feel tense. She hated pain unless it involved him holding onto her during sex.

"Tell me if it hurts too much. I'll stop if you can't stand it, Kels."

Muttering her response she waited to feel his cock. His hands were smooth, no trace of the gel, and he must have wiped the excess off somewhere. He spread the cheeks of her ass wide, and then his hands withdrew.

Licking her lips as nerves got the better of her, Kelsey felt his cock touch her anus. She jumped, jerking away from his touch. Feeling silly, she settled back down with her ass in the air.

"Trust me, Kels. I've never made this bad for you before."

She couldn't argue. There was no way for her to blame him for her lost virginity. For anyone it would have been painful.

"Relax," he said.

He pushed the tip to her ass, and she gasped at the pressure he placed on her anus.

"Touch yourself," Killer ordered her, and she reached between her thighs to touch her clit. From the first caress of her clit she felt herself melt.

One of his hands touched her hip as the other must have been holding his cock to guide into her.

She imagined him gripping the base of the shaft,

ready to feed the tip into her ass. Her thoughts alone turned her on, and she wanted him more than anything.

The tip of his cock opened her up, sliding inside.

"You've got the head, baby. How does it feel?" he asked, both hands going to her hips.

"Weird."

He chuckled, caressing her hips as inch by inch he fed his cock into her body. She couldn't deny the pleasure that came with the pain of his cock. Her ass burned with every inch he fed inside her.

She didn't tell him to stop, waiting to see if he was right about her loving it. Gripping the blanket, she tried to hold onto something. His cock was not thin or short. Every part of him was large, and she knew if she wasn't careful, she wouldn't be able to sit down tomorrow.

"Almost there," he said, soothing her.

"Please." She'd spoken that word more in the last few days than she ever had through her whole life.

Seconds later he shushed her. She didn't know she'd been moaning aloud. "You've got it all, Kels. I'm inside. I'm not going anywhere."

Breathing out, she became aware of the pleasure storming her body. She'd gone from not feeling anything to being taken over by nothing but sheer lust.

"Come for me, baby. Keep playing with your clit."

She worked her clit as he moved in and out of her ass. Kelsey was thankful he took his time, drawing their pleasure out. He wasn't rushed in his movements to fuck her ass.

Reaching her climax through touching her clit, she splintered apart at the same time Killer picked up the tempo of his thrusts. He fucked her hard but steadily never breaking the barrier of pleasure into unbearable pain.

"So fucking perfect, I love you, Kels." He screamed the words, and she felt his cock jerk within her. They both collapsed to the bed, but Killer wouldn't give her time to get her breath back.

He carried her into the bath, washing away the evidence of what they'd done together. When he was finished, he carried her back to bed, sliding under the covers. The night was far from over. Killer wasn't in a rush to try anything else. He wrapped his arms around her, holding her close to him.

"Killer?" she asked, thinking about Fort Wills and the life they both had.

"Yeah, baby."

"Do you think everything is going to be all right?" She glanced behind her to see his closed off expression. Kelsey hated it when he did that.

"I don't know if everything is going to be all right, but I do know I'll protect you no matter what." He kissed her temple.

As far as answers went, she hated it. There was nothing either of them could do to help. Either way, she hated feeling helpless. Killer was going to protect her, but how was she going to protect him?

****

Michael stood outside of The Skulls compound waiting for someone to come and see him. Daniel had phoned ahead and arranged for a meeting. No one would open the gate to let him inside. He saw the car from the picture Daniel had shown him some hours ago. What the fuck would he do if his woman and a Skull were killed?

The door to the clubhouse opened, and Tiny made his way toward the gate, followed by Lash, Nash, and Zero. The men took their time looking ready to do murder. Michael also spotted the weapons in their hands.

They were not going to mess around.

He hated this world, and the sooner he got rid of everything the better it would be.

"What the fuck are you doing here?" Tiny asked.

"We've got problems, and I need to talk to you."

"I know what problems you got. I warned you if any women went missing from my town then I'd come to you. I've got everything I need to get rid of you, you piece of shit." Tiny slammed his palm over a button, sliding the gate open.

Within seconds he was trapped against Tiny's body with a gun poised at his temple. Daniel along with another guard climbed out of the car aiming a gun at Tiny. Lash, Nash, and Zero had their pieces pointed at his men. This meeting was turning into a fucking catastrophe.

"Three girls. Three fucking teenage girls have gone missing from my town. One blonde, one a brunette, and the other a fucking redhead. You want to tell it's a coincidence?" Tiny's voice was raised. From the sound of it, Tiny was ready to end him. Michael gritted his teeth fighting against the fear.

"I haven't taken them," Michael said. "This is not about me or the fucking girls. Killer and Kelsey are in danger."

He squeezed the words out through the tight grip around his throat.

"Boss, I think he's telling the truth," Nash said.

Tiny tightened his hold then threw him to the ground. The barrel of the gun was still trained on him. "You better start fucking talking, or tonight will see the end of you."

Holding his hands up, Michael explained everything. For the first time since finding out his heritage he told Tiny all, including his disgust and what he'd been trying to do to get the girls taken elsewhere. Michael couldn't save them all, but he tried.

By the time he was finished the men were on their cell phones trying to get in touch with Killer.

The other Skull wasn't answering his phone, and if Michael was right, his enemy was already there to take Kelsey. He'd failed her.

Chapter Fifteen

Killer debated putting his cell phone on to charge up. The phone was completely dead, and he'd forgotten to charge it up last night. Deciding against it, he headed downstairs to find Kelsey standing at the stove cooking breakfast. She wore a lovely blue summer dress only this time she'd left the cardigan in the wardrobe. It was a hot summer, and wearing any clothes was a chore.

Throwing the phone onto the table he went to make himself a coffee.

"Have they called?" she asked, turning toward him. Last night had been one of the best nights of his life. He'd never had so much fun before. Kelsey was so responsive to his touch. Her adventurous side matched his own.

"No, I'm going to leave it today. I don't want to be interrupted." He poured them both a coffee watching her flip some bacon in a frying pan. Killer never thought he'd love the domestic feel to his life. Kelsey made him want stuff he never thought he did.

"What are you thinking?" she asked, pressing a finger to his frowning brows. Taking her hand, he kissed her palm before moving back to the table.

"Nothing much. I just enjoy being here with you. It's fun."

She nodded, serving up their breakfast. "Is it wise to leave the phone dead? What if they want to get in touch with you?" They'd both agreed to not have a landline in case someone recognized their voice. Whizz had been the one to warn him about sound recognition.

"Yeah, you're right," he said, picking the phone up. "I'll eat this and then go and put it on charge."

He pocketed the phone and smiled at her.

There was a healthy glow to her cheeks. Last

night had brought them closer, if that was at all possible.

"You're going to make me blush if you keep looking at me like that."

"I can't help it. You know what I'm thinking about?" he asked, grabbing her hand.

"Do I want to know?"

He shook his head, smiling. "Probably not."

She laughed. "I've never seen you like this before."

Killer waited for her to elaborate.

"Fine, you're always so quiet, and you never really talk or smile. I mean, it's not a bad thing to see you smile, but I've never seen you so happy not even when we were dating." She bit her lip and looked down at her breakfast.

Squeezing her hand he tried to offer her comfort. "I've never had a reason to be happy. I know the time we've spent together has been all over the place. We've never dated, Kels. My past, it's pretty fucking dark." He stopped recalling all the order from the leader of The Lions. Gritting his teeth he forced the memories down, refusing to let himself be vulnerable. "I promise myself the moment I got into The Skulls I'd never kill anyone unless I could guarantee they were guilty or if they hurt those I care about."

They were silent, and he dropped the fork onto his plate, losing his appetite.

"We don't need to discuss this, Killer. I'm so sorry. I meant by words how happy you are, and I hope it's because of me as much as this set-up."

Seeing her concern lightened his mood. He kept hold of her hand like a lifeline. "I killed people, Kels. I killed men and women. Whores, criminal, and innocents." He turned to look off to the side. The remembered screams still haunted him if he allowed them in. "That is my past, baby. It's the past, and I'm not going to let it affect our future."

"I know." She climbed off her chair and sat down on his lap. "Your past is staying there." Kelsey cupped his face. "I love you, Killer. Not the man you were." She kissed his lips.

He held onto her waist knowing he'd found heaven inside her. "What did I ever do to deserve you?" he asked.

"You stuck around." She kissed his lips, chuckling. "Go, charge your phone, and see what home has to say. I want to make this real in Fort Wills."

She climbed off him, taking their food to the sink.

Leaving her alone, he walked upstairs to find the charger on the vanity table. Inserting the cable into the phone, he plugged it into the wall and turned the blasted thing on. He hated cell phones and had a tendency to break them. Why did companies have to keep bringing out a smaller device that was flimsier than the last?

Within seconds the phone rang. Glancing down he saw it was Tiny calling. Accepting the call, he pressed the device to his ear. "What's the matter?" he asked.

"Killer, fuck, why haven't you been answering the fucking phone?" Tate asked. Hearing Tiny's daughter instead of the man unnerved him.

"What the hell are you doing with his phone?" Looking toward the door, he frowned, listening for Kelsey's humming. Whenever she washed dishes she hummed to herself.

"Tiny and the boys are on their way. The shit has hit the fan. Get Kelsey, and get out of there. It's too dangerous. Michael Granito is not the problem. His enemies are after her to blackmail him."

He dropped the phone, heading downstairs. Grabbing the keys from the drawer beside the door, he called Kelsey's name out. She didn't answer his call. Grabbing the gun he kept in the drawer for safe keeping he called her name out again.

Frowning, he made his way down the corridor. Taking the safety off the gun he rounded the corner, and it took every ounce of strength not to fall apart. One man held Kelsey in his arms with a knife pressed to her neck. A second man held her wrist out and was opening up her wound. The third man had a gun pressed to her temple. The fear in her eyes would stay with him forever. He'd left her for a few seconds, and three men he'd never seen held her against her will, threatening her.

"Who the fuck are you?" he asked, shouting the words.

He held the gun up waiting for the right opportunity to kill them. If he fired at any of them the other would harm or kill her. Fuck, he couldn't protect her.

"We're none of your concern," the one with the knife said.

"The moment you touched my woman, you became my concern," he said, glaring between them.

"Your woman? This is Michael Granito's woman, and we need her."

Teeth gritted he looked Kelsey in the eye. Tears fell down her face cutting him to the core.

Come on, Killer. You can do this. They're nothing.

"Michael has got no hold over her. Let her go and take your shit out on him." He needed to keep them in this house. Fucking small house and he didn't have any of his brothers to help him.

"No, we know he'll become more amenable with her help."

"You're wrong," Kelsey said, speaking up. She

cried out as the guy holding the knife pressed it against her throat tighter.

"Did I give you permission to fucking speak?"

Blood dripped down from the blade.

"She means nothing to him. Why the fuck are you bothering with her?" Killer asked, feeling helpless. He'd never been helpless in his life, and yet there was nothing he could do.

"Any man in our world who keeps their woman a secret is important," Knife guy said. "She'll be perfect for what we want, and then we'll sell her."

If they left the house then he was fucked. Finding Kelsey would be impossible if they tried to sell her. Men like them wouldn't give a fuck about her. They would sell her to turn over a profit. "No, you're not leaving here."

He was laughed at. His anger spiked at their mocking.

"You're in no position to bargain with us." The knife guy nodded to the man at her wrist.

She screamed as the knife dragged over the wound that had been healing. Blood seeped out of the wound.

"Let her the fuck go!" He yelled the words, forcing himself to hold back from what was happening.

Blood fell from her wrist to drop on the floor.

Turning his gun he tensed on the trigger. He didn't fire, and only wished he could.

"You're Killer, right? Why don't you join us? We pay a lot of money, and the women are easy to come by. They'll do everything to stop the pain."

Kelsey whimpered.

Shaking his head, he gritted his teeth knowing he needed to make a choice. He either fired at one and risked the other two killing her, or he let them walk out, hoping no harm came to her. Both choices were fucking shit ones.

"I love you," she said, mouthing the words so no one could see but him.

No, he wasn't saying goodbye, and her words felt like a goodbye. Shaking his head, he stared at the others. None of them left him a choice.

When he was about to let down his weapon he heard a shot ring out, and the man with the gun at her head fell down. He didn't give himself time to panic, only to react. Firing his gun he dropped the other two men, and Kelsey collapsed in a heap. Noise filled the house as more men came around the front. He went down to the floor, turning and holding his gun up.

Thank fuck he didn't fire as he was staring at Tiny, leader of The Skulls.

Throwing the gun away, he went to Kelsey's side. Her wrist was bleeding, and he wrapped her wrist with a towel.

"I've got you, baby."

She had a cut at her throat.

"What the hell is going on?" he asked, turning back to Tiny. He paused seeing Michael standing beside him. "You?" Reaching for his gun he had the other man trapped against the wall.

Within seconds two guns were trained on him, and his brothers had guns trained on the men.

"Are you going to kill me?" Michael asked.

"Killer, man, let him go. We'll tell you everything," Tiny said, putting a hand on his shoulder.

"He's responsible for hurting my woman."

"No, he's not. Please, we've got to get you out of here and deal with this mess." Tiny kept talking, but all Killer wanted to do was kill Michael.

"Killer, help me please," Kelsey said.

Her pain-filled voice got through to him.

Withdrawing, he glared at the other man, but he walked away. Kelsey needed him a lot more than this fucker needed to die.

Picking Kelsey up, he walked out of the house.
****

One day later

Kelsey sat in bed waiting for some visitors. Killer hadn't taken his time to get her to the Fort Wills hospital. He had initially taken her to the hospital in Paradise Rocks. She didn't like it, and after they'd bound up her hands, she'd asked for him to bring her back to Fort Wills. Breaking most of the speed laws, he'd been determined to get her here. He picked her up off the hospital bed and carried her out to the car. Without waiting for an explanation he drove the couple of hours to get back into their old town. He would do anything she asked. Sandy came to her to check over the damage Michael's enemies created. No one had stopped them not even to take down her insurance details.

She tucked some hair behind her ear hoping she didn't see the inside of a hospital any time soon after this latest turn. It was Sunday, and she wanted to be discharged today.

Tate knocked at the door, looking around the corner to smile at her.

"Hey," Kelsey said, climbing off the bed to embrace her friend.

"I was so fucking worried about you. God, when Killer came to the clubhouse looking ready to murder someone." Tate cupped her cheek, smiling. "I'm so pleased you're alive. When Michael came around we were all worried."

Sitting down on the bed, Kelsey listened to Tate talk, catching up on everything they missed.

"How about you?" Tate asked, picking up her bandaged arm. "Is everything okay with you?"

"Are you asking me if I'm going to kill myself at the first opportunity?"

"I won't be giving her the chance." Killer spoke up from the doorway. He stood, leaning against the frame. "Hey, baby," he said.

"Hey, yourself." Her heart pounded at the sight of him. "I thought you'd forgotten about me."

"Never forget about you." He stepped toward her, taking her hand and kissing her knuckles. "I had some business to take care of."

"Well I'm going to leave you to it. I know my dad and the others are already back, so I'm off to be nosy." Tate hugged her close before moving away. "I'm glad you're back, honey. I'll book us a day at the beauty salon. We'll be back to our old selves in no time."

Laughing, Kelsey watched her friend leave before turning her attention back to Killer.

"You look all serious. Do I want to know what's been going on without me there?" she asked.

"I've been talking with Alex. I've got everything I need to get Michael Granito out of your life for good." Killer sighed, sitting down on the bed beside her.

"What's the matter? You don't look happy about that." She started to worry. Did he no longer want her after everything they'd been through?

He took hold of her hand, locking their fingers together. "I don't care about your parents. You never talk about them, and I know you're not sad to not see them." She licked her lips feeling nervous. Her parents were part of the past. They'd never been in contact with them since she left. "Michael, away from the trafficking, he's rich, Kels."

"What are you trying to say?"

"I love you. I've never been more sure of anything in my life than the way I feel about you." Killer cupped her cheek. "But I can't give you a rich life. I've got enough money to make us comfortable."

Breathing out a sigh, she smiled.

"He can give you the fancy house, the jet-setting lifestyle. You can have it all."

Pressing a finger to his lips, Kelsey shook her head. "Shut up." Thinking of her words carefully, she stared into his dark brown gaze. "For the last eight years I could have lived that life. I work as a dental nurse. I live within my means in a small apartment. Killer, I don't want what he's offering. I'm not in love with him. I've never been in live with anyone but you." She kissed his lips, feeling them harden beneath her touch. "If you don't want me, then fine, but don't push me away offering me more than what I want."

Killer pushed her to the bed, slamming his lips down on hers. "Good, because this was your last chance to go. You're not leaving my side no matter what."

Several minutes later the nurse walked in cursing them. Any other time Kelsey would have been embarrassed by what was going on. Having Killer by her side, she didn't care. Later that day she was released from the hospital with an appointment to see a physiatrist. Kelsey would talk to the woman even though she didn't feel it was necessary.

Tate was waiting with Angel and Sophia outside of the hospital.

"What's going on?" she asked.

"I've got some club business to attend to, and then I'll be coming back to your apartment. They're going to get you settled. Lavish you with love and gossip."

"Are you sure I can't convince you to stay?"

Kelsey asked. She wanted to be alone with her man.

"No, business comes first, baby." He held her hand as they made their way to the waiting car. "I'm leaving her in your good hands. Make sure she's in one piece when I get her back."

"Giant, we're not going anywhere to hurt her." Tate winked at him.

Laughing, Kelsey climbed in the backseat while the others got into the car. The children were being looked after by Eva at the big house.

She watched him climb on the back of his bike as they drove away.

"Everything will be back to normal in no time," Sophia said, drawing her attention away from the window.

"One thing you've got to learn, honey, being an old lady you've got to get used to club business. Isn't that right, girls?" Tate asked.

They all hummed in agreement.

"You can either be part of it and get your man to share everything, or you can pretend it doesn't exist." Tate kept talking, distracting her.

"Lash tells me what I need to know. I love him. The Skulls is his business," Angel said.

"I, on the other hand, demand to know everything from Murphy."

"Same here. Nash is not keeping anything from me," Sophia said.

"He kind of has to. Tiny is still making him pee in cups," Tate pointed out.

"Yeah, and has he failed any tests? No, because I keep him part of my business."

The girls talked between themselves, and Kelsey thought about Killer. She wondered what was more important than taking her home? Did she want to know about club business?

Rubbing her temples, she knew deep down, she didn't care about any business as long as Killer was with her, in her arms for the rest of their lives.

****

Entering the clubhouse, Killer stared around at his fellow brothers. They were all waiting for him. Michael along with two of his guards sat on chairs in the center of the room. He knew since leaving Paradise Rocks that The Skulls had dealt with the mess of the dead bodies including the men doing the trafficking.

Alex held a file in his hands. Killer already knew what it contained. Details, pictures, reports linking Michael to the trafficking organization. This was only one area. They all knew trafficking went far beyond the rich businessman in front of him.

"Tate taking care of your woman?" Murphy asked.

"Yeah, she's on her way back to her apartment." Killer glanced toward Tiny, who simply looked back at him.

"He's all yours."

Grabbing a chair, he straddled it looking at Michael. "Don't talk. We know who you are. We also know how you started up and how the trafficking business fell into your hands." Killer wished he could hate the other man. Everything he learned about Michael, he knew the other man cared about Kelsey to a point, trying to keep her safe even as he put her in danger. Still, there was no love, and he'd used her to get what he wanted. "We've got the proof of your involvement." Alex stepped forward, opening the file giving Michael time to see. "You owe us. Right now you can get out of the trafficking business. Give us the details of the women taken and become an informant for the law."

The Skulls didn't want anything to do with the slave trade. Tiny had two daughters, not to mention all of the women in their lives. There was no way they'd ever support that kind of business.

"You also divorce Kelsey and stay the fuck out of her life."

"If I don't do either?" Michael asked, after being given permission to talk.

"We've got everything we need to get rid of you. You either do as we ask, or you leave, but we'll get our way."

"You got the law on your hands?"

"My woman has," Tiny said, speaking up. "Her father knows men who can land you right in shit. I think you'd make some big guy's bitch in jail. Your ass will be really nice and open by the time they are done with you."

The threat was clear.

Michael smiled. "You don't think I've got the same information on you? A lot of people have died because of you."

Killer stood up, taking a step back.

"The difference between us is we've got men on the inside. The Skulls are far and wide. Some of our members are in prison, fuck-head," Zero said. "You wouldn't last five minutes whereas we'd have a very comfortable stay. Our only worries would be getting too comfortable."

The other members laughed. Killer saw the humor even though he didn't want to test it. Kelsey was his woman, and he didn't want to leave her for a cell.

"Sir, I think you should consider it. They're giving you an out." One of his guards started talking.

For several minutes silence fell on the room. Killer waited for his answer.

After some time passed, Michael finally nodded.

Alex left the room starting to make arrangements. The divorce papers were already set up. Tate had given them to him earlier. Her lawyer friend had drawn them up.

Michael sighed, letting gout a breath. "You better treat her with care."

"She'll want for nothing," Killer said. He handed the papers back to Tiny, promising to deal with them.

When everything was finished, he left the clubhouse and headed to her apartment. The girls left as he arrived, and he was alone with his woman.

"You're a divorced woman, baby," he said, kissing her head.

"What?"

"Michael is going to be out of our lives. We're free."

She jumped on him, laughing and giggling.

Carrying her toward the bedroom, Killer kicked the door shut, happy to have his world back in one piece.

Chapter Sixteen

Nine months later

Killer stared out over the garden watching as Kelsey continued to pull the weeds out of the vegetable patch she insisted on. He looked at the ring on his finger and couldn't stop smiling. They had been married three months ago in church. Tate had organized a white wedding with all the right decorations that any woman would wish for.

For their honeymoon he took Kelsey to Vegas where they spent all their time in the hotel room, making love, fucking, and being together. He'd finally gotten the chance to feel her naked heat around his shaft.

The psychiatrist had discharged her, happy that she was no longer going to try to hurt herself. He had no doubt about their feelings.

Tiny and Eva's wedding present to them had been this house. The modest three bedroom detached house was a dream. Killer didn't know if he could handle living in a house paid for by his club leader. The moment Kelsey saw the place and seeing her love for it, Killer knew he'd learn to accept the gift.

Watching her body wrapped in a sweater and jeans, he got rock hard. It was spring, and the weather was all over the place.

She looked up, smiling at him and waving back at him. They were due at Tiny's place for their usual Sunday lunch. Eva was cooking a large feast for all of them. He scented the casserole in the oven that Kelsey was taking.

All of the women always brought their own choice of dish. Eva would be swamped with leftovers for the club.

Heading outside to their garden, he helped her up, removing the gloves on her hands to reveal the gold ring he bought her. Throughout the week she still worked as a dental nurse, and the weekends were theirs.

"How is our vegetable patch coming?" he asked.

"It's early, but I reckon we could get some great produce this year." She went on her toes, claiming his lips. "How is my husband today?"

The smile on her face was infectious.

"Feeling satisfied." He drew her closer to him, rubbing his cock against her stomach. "What about my wife?"

"Aching in all the good ways."

Kelsey had stuck to his rules. Whenever she needed him, she sought him out for him to take care of her needs. He would never forget the way she'd walked into the clubhouse one Friday night and sat on his lap. She straddled his cock, leaned forward and whispered against his ear, telling him everything that was wrong with her body. He took the whole night trying to give her everything she needed.

"Baby, you keep talking like that and we're not going to leave this house for a good long time."

She rubbed his cock making him moan. "Why do we have to leave?" she asked.

He was tempted to cancel, but he knew how much Eva worked for them. "When we get home, I'll fuck you until you're screaming my name. I promise."

They walked into their home, laughing. He waited for her to grab the casserole from the oven and cover it. Killer took the car as he had nowhere to put the casserole on his bike. Kelsey hummed beside him, looking out of the window.

In the last nine months Kelsey had gotten her divorce, married Killer, and was no longer connected to

Michael Granito in any way. The old ladies had taken her under their wing, drawing her back into club business. He loved seeing her at all the barbeques relaxing with all The Skulls.

On the other hand, Michael was working with the law in trying to break the trafficking pool. Alex at all club meetings kept them informed of his whereabouts. Eva's father, Ned, also kept an eye on him. The leader of the fighters made sure his daughter was protected at every turn.

Arriving at Eva's house, Killer cut the engine smiling at all the bikes in the driveway.

"Wow, it's going to be a full house today," Kelsey said.

"Yeah, Sunday lunch always is."

He placed a hand on her back, walking with her to the front door. They walked straight inside without even bothering to knock. The commotion hit them right in the face. Tate passed them, smiling and taking Kelsey's hand. "Stealing your woman."

Before he got a chance to say anything to her, Killer was left alone. The table was laid for all of them. He saw Eva and Sophia working the kitchen, getting everything ready. Heading outside he found the rest of the men, smoking, talking, and drinking.

Shaking hands with most of them, he headed toward Tiny, Lash, Nash, and Murphy. Zero stood with them as well, but the other brother looked troubled.

"Where's Kelsey?" Zero asked.

"Tate stole her. I swear if Tate had a dick I'd worry to never get my wife back," Killer said, joking.

"My woman doesn't have a problem with dick."

Tiny lashed out, which Murphy ducked, laughing.

"Sorry, man, I keep forgetting."

"Let's not talk about my daughter and her habits

behind closed doors. I don't need to know what she gets up to."

Lighting up a cigarette, Killer blew the smoke up to the sky. He listened to the men talk all around him. Killer was content to simply be part of it all.

"Any news on Mason Terry?" Nash asked.

Mason Terry had been the man to take out one of the guys hurting Kelsey.

"Yeah, he doesn't' want to come to Fort Wills. He likes his own life in Paradise Rocks, but if we ever need him again, he's more than happy to help."

Killer made a note to call the other man to thank him once again.

No amount of thanks would ever make up for Kelsey's life. She meant the world to him, and he made sure everyone knew it.

"Dinner!" Eva yelled out of the back door for them all to hear. He stayed back, waiting for the other men to charge forward.

"Anyone would think they've not been fed," Zero said.

"They probably haven't."

Killer made his way inside and saw Kelsey already sat at the table.

He kissed Kelsey's head as he pulled out his chair to sit. Sitting beside her he saw Tate and Murphy were opposite them. Dinner started, and dishes and plates were handed around. He made sure to fill his own plate along with Kelsey's.

"Make sure you fill her plate up," Tate said, speaking up.

The whole table went silent.

"What?" he asked, looking from Kelsey to Tate.

"Nothing. She means nothing," Kelsey said, glaring at Tate.

Eva was chuckling along with Tiny. What joke wasn't he getting?

"You're going to have to tell him."

"You did this on purpose!" Kelsey turned to him. He saw she forced a smile.

"Is something wrong? Are you ill?" he asked, panicking.

"No, I'm not ill, but I'm going to be sick in the mornings for some time."

"What?" He was missing something.

"I'm pregnant, Killer. We're going to have a little boy or girl. A baby."

"Pregnant?"

"Yes, I was going to tell you when I was sure." She shot an accusatory glare at Tate. "However, someone took that away from me."

"How sure can you get with a pregnancy test kit? You've taken one, and you just wanted to confirm with a doctor," Tate asked.

Sinking to his knees, he pulled out her chair, resting a palm to her stomach. "We're going to have a baby?"

"Yes, are you happy?"

Pulling her to her feet, Killer cupped her face. The entire room blew up in applause, whistles, and joy. He was going to be a father. Fear, happiness, excitement, nervousness, all of those feelings washed over him, but not once did he regret getting her pregnant. His wife was pregnant with his child.

Sitting down to dinner, he got slapped on the back and cheers from all the men while the women congratulated Kelsey. *A family*. They were going to be a big happy family. Shit, what was he going to do when it came to her giving birth?

He recalled Tiny's reaction to Eva. Fuck, he

wasn't going to be able to handle it. Kelsey squeezed his hand, and he calmed. Whatever happened, they'd get through it together.

****

Kelsey squealed as the moment they entered their home, Killer picked her up and carried her upstairs. From the moment Tate had spilled the beans, he'd been so attentive. Killer was always attentive, but something felt different. His touch to her stomach was tender. The love shining from his eyes made her heart stop.

"We're going to be parents," he said, crouching down in front of her.

"Are you sure you're happy with the news?" she asked, biting her lip and feeling nervous.

"Baby, I can't begin to describe how you make me feel." He tilted her head back, kissing her lips.

Moaning, she opened up for his invasion, loving the way he deepened the kiss.

They fought each other to remove their clothes. In no time at all they were naked, and Killer held her to the bed, stopping her from moving anywhere but where he wanted her.

"You're mine, Kels."

"I've always been yours," she said, moaning. His lips captured one of her nipples, sucking on the tip hard.

Heat filled her pussy, and the need to come swamped her. Killer slid inside her without a condom. They'd been making love for a long time without any protection. She hadn't given contraception a thought.

They were going to have a family all of their own.

He held her hands beside her head, staring down at her. She gazed into his eyes never wanting to be anywhere but with him.

"You've made me one of the happiest men in the

world," he said, pulling out only to press back inside her.

She cried out, feeling him hit her deep inside. Thrusting up, she met him with every stroke. He pounded inside her, drawing two orgasms from her before he finally joined her into bliss.

He collapsed over her, panting for breath. Kelsey didn't want him to move, but after a few seconds he pulled away, to cup her cheek. The intensity of his gaze made her heart race.

"I'm the luckiest man in the world."

"I'm not the only woman who can get pregnant," she said, smiling.

"Not talking about the baby. I love *you*. The baby is just a bonus, but you, you're the one who makes me the luckiest man in the world."

His words took her by surprise. Her only response was to grab his face and kiss the life out of him. Kelsey was the lucky woman. Not many women could have a man willing to leave their club behind to keep her safe.

Eight months later, Kelsey smiled as Killer looked down at the son she had given birth to. Now they were a complete family. The love she saw on his face was similar to the love shining in his eyes whenever he looked at her.

Epilogue

From the end of Devil's Charm

Zero parked his bike up for the night and charged into the club house. He'd just gotten back from the barbeque Devil had hosted at his house in Piston County. A beer and a woman to fuck were what he needed. Spending the whole day watching Sophia with Nash had driven him insane.

No matter how many women he fucked, he couldn't stop the feelings she evoked within him. Fucking woman was going to send him into an early grave. Part of him had been tempted to cut away from the club and head up to Paradise Rocks to get to know Mason Terry.

Heading outside around the back of the clubhouse, he heard all of the men getting back into the club. The kids were screaming their tiredness. Some of the men took off going to their homes. Killer, along with a couple of others, hadn't been to the barbeque.

Resting his head against the brick, Zero tried to get *her* out of his thoughts. The only time he stopped thinking about her was when he was alone with Prue. He went to visit her regularly as it was getting closer to the anniversary of her brother's death.

Blowing out a breath, he took a large gulp of his beer.

Someone was close beside him, and he turned to see the woman of his nightmares standing there, smiling.

"What the fuck are you doing here?" he asked, staring at Sophia. The smile dropped from her lips.

"I came to see if you were all right. Nash was worried."

Fucking man was begging to start a fight over

her.

"What do you want? All I want is some peace away from you. Is that so hard to ask?" He growled the words out. Smashing the bottle onto the floor, he caught her arms. "Don't you see I'm trying here?"

"Zero, you're scaring me," she said.

"Fuck it, you know what? I've been a good boy up until now, but you're everywhere. I can't get away from you." Zero was going straight to hell, but he was going to have a taste of heaven before he went.

Drawing her closer, he felt her tense but didn't give a shit. He needed her sweet lips on him.

"Zero, stop, you don't want to do this," she said.

He fucking did and was going to finally do what he'd been craving. Lowering his head down, he was a breath away when a scream, the sound of a gunshot, and men shouting surrounded them. Covering Sophia, he looked around waiting to see what had happened.

"What was that?" he asked, forgetting all about kissing her.

His brothers were shouting out orders, calling for Sandy. Together they left the back of the clubhouse to see what all the fuss was about.

Zero stopped when he saw the dark red hair. He recognized that shade of hair. Butch held the woman's head in his lap, barking out orders. Charging through the group, Zero felt his world finally shatter. Blood coated Prue's front near her heart. Her eyes were wide and terrified as she stared at him.

He saw her mouth open as she coughed, more blood coming out of her mouth.

"He's back," she said, struggling with every word. In her hand was a picture, and he took it staring down at the old school picture of him, Prue, and her brother. Ten years ago, he had been responsible for her brother's death. He'd never caught the bastard who put the bullet in his best friend's gut, killing him slowly. Looking at the back he saw the message.

"Two down, one to go."

Prue gasped for breath. The one person he'd sworn to protect was dying in front of him. Zero looked around feeling lost. Prue had been the only lifeline he had. Pressing his hands to her wounds, he prayed she survived.

He wasn't going to lose another person he loved. In that one moment, Zero knew he had a limited amount of time left. Someone had a target on his head, and it was up to him to find out who.

The End

www.samcrescent.com

EVERNIGHT PUBLISHING ®

www.evernightpublishing.com

CPSIA information can be obtained
at www.ICGtesting.com
Printed in the USA
LVHW040055190419
614781LV00001B/22

9 781773 395609